'You're too generous for your own good, Lara.

'Let me put yo_____ _____ __an I am, in case you _____ I'm somehow better _____ _____hers. I'm a taker—n_____ _____kind of world I inhabit the weak fall by the wayside and are quickly forgotten. I've had to learn to be tough. On the road to achieving what I want I've learned not to let anything or anyone stand in my way. If I come back int_ _our life again I'm guaranteed to hurt you an_ ____e you rue the day you met me.'

'_____ __ if I_ _____ng some kind _____... Don't worry about that, Gabriel. I'm ne___ ___ sniffed and wrenched her arm free.

'Is that right?'

In a flash Gabriel was on his feet and bringing her up towards him, moving his hands down to her slim waist to hold her fast and pulling her against the iron wall of his chest.

Then the world as she knew it disappeared as though it was nothing but a hazy dream and her eyelids shut tight as he crushed her lips beneath his. The frightening demand she sensed left Lara reeling. But it also stirred long-dormant feelings in her body, making them want to rise up and meet that furious hunger.

The day **Maggie Cox** saw the film version of *Wuthering Heights*, with a beautiful Merle Oberon and a very handsome Laurence Olivier, was the day she became hooked on romance. From that day onwards she spent a lot of time dreaming up her own romances, secretly hoping that one day she might become published and get paid for doing what she loved most! Now that her dream is being realised she wakes up every morning and counts her blessings. She is married to a gorgeous man and is the mother of two wonderful sons. Her two other great passions in life—besides her family and reading/writing—are music and films.

Recent titles by the same author:

THE TYCOON'S DELICIOUS DISTRACTION
WHAT HIS MONEY CAN'T HIDE
DISTRACTED BY HER
A DEVILISHLY DARK DEAL

THE MAN
SHE CAN'T FORGET

BY
MAGGIE COX

Published in Great Britain 2014
by Mills & Boon, an imprint of Harlequin (UK) Limited,
Eton House, 18-24 Paradise Road, Richmond, Surrey, TW9 1SR

© 2014 Maggie Cox

ISBN: 978 0 263 90864 0

Harlequin (UK) Limited's policy is to use papers that are natural,
renewable and recyclable products and made from wood grown in
sustainable forests. The logging and manufacturing processes conform
to the legal environmental regulations of the country of origin.

Printed and bound in Spain
by Blackprint CPI, Barcelona

THE MAN
SHE CAN'T FORGET

CHAPTER ONE

IT HAD SEEMED like a good idea at the time. If only Lara
had remembered her brother Sean's sage advice to 'expect the unexpected', then she might have thought twice
about agreeing to stay at their parents' home while they
took a much needed restorative break in the south of
France.

But then Sean wasn't there any more to remind her
of that particular little pearl....

And, in truth, she would never have dreamt of re-
fusing her mum and dad's request to house-sit for them
when they were still reeling from the tragedy that had
hit them all six months ago. *Their son, Sean, Lara's
brother, was dead.* He had contracted malaria whilst
undertaking the charity work that he loved in Africa
and had not recovered from it. It hardly seemed real
that such a thing was possible in the twenty-first century, but sadly it was.

Having already been back in the family home for
a week now, Lara still expected him to walk through
the door with a cheery, 'Put the kettle on, sis, I could
murder a cup of tea!' just like he had done when they
were teenagers.

Time seemed intent on playing tricks on her these

days. One minute it passed like a slow and choking mudslide, threatening to cut off her ability to breathe, and the next... The next it seemed to vanish completely, leaving her feeling that she was stuck in a desolate and unhappy dream that she couldn't wake up from.

Whilst she loved her work, she was glad that the college term had come to an end. Her duties and responsibilities in the library had been particularly arduous this past month, what with so many students wanting help with research to take home with them. But now that that frenetic time was over she had no choice but to fully embrace her grief and process the soul-deep pain that she felt at losing Sean.

But, truthfully, she didn't relish the prospect of the endless summer days stretching ahead of her as she normally would have done. With nothing to lighten her mood but the daily walks she would go on with Barney, her parents' devoted Border Terrier, Lara had been dreading the time to be spent alone at her parents' house.

She could have arranged to go on holiday herself when they returned from France, but she hadn't had the heart for it. A couple of friends had asked her to join them on a trip to Italy but she'd declined. How could she possibly be good company when she was still grieving so badly for Sean?

Now, in the middle of her second week's stay at the family home, Lara was sitting at the sturdy oak kitchen table, making a half-hearted attempt at eating a bowl of unappetising breakfast cereal, when the doorbell rang. Such a lyrical bell-like sound shouldn't pierce her to the very core, but it did. In fact it made her flinch. She seemed to be afraid of everything these days. But Sean being taken from them so suddenly like that had made her fear that nothing good would ever happen to her or her family again.

Rousing himself from the relaxed position he'd assumed, lying across her feet, Barney shot up and started barking and wagging his tail—just as though he was anticipating a welcome friend or visitor. Lara's nerves were jangled even more. It was eight-thirty in the morning.... Who on earth would be calling at this time?

'For goodness' sake,' she muttered beneath her breath, 'it's probably just the postman.'

Forcing herself to relax, she moved down the hardwood hallway in her bare feet, Barney eagerly following her. The day was already promising to be particularly warm, and the sun that shone through the door's decorated Victorian glass panes lit up the interior with the glare of a powerful spotlight.

Lifting her hand to shield her gaze, she squinted at the tall shadow behind the glass. Even though she didn't have a clue who it was she knew it wasn't the postman. Whoever it was, his straight, ominous stance suggested someone official. Lara's stomach executed a nervous cartwheel. *Please, God, not more bad news.*

She opened the door warily. 'Good morning.'

On the other side of the door stood a man with eyes so heartbreakingly blue that the sight of them made her catch her breath. Waves of disconcerting shock flooded her. Staring at the carved, high-cheekboned visage, with its cut-glass jaw and arresting dimple, Lara thought she was dreaming. To be confronted by the man that she'd thought never to see again, and so early in the morning, she found she was both lost for words and stunned right down to her marrow.

He was dressed in an exquisitely tailored dark suit with a dulled gold pinstripe, and the clearly custom-made clothing showed off her visitor's athletic, broad-shouldered physique to perfection. He had always looked classy, even when he was a student. Some people were just born with that exclusive air about them and this man was one of them.

As the sexy, expensive cologne he wore wafted tantalisingly beneath her nose she wanted to pinch herself, just to make sure she wasn't dreaming.

Her visitor proffered a tentative smile and she immediately sensed his uneasiness, as though for a disconcerting moment he wasn't sure what the appropriate greeting was.

'I was wondering if I might have a word with Mr or Mrs Bradley?' he asked. 'I'm a— I *was* a friend of theirs. I'm sorry I'm calling so early in the morning, but I've just got back from New York and I wanted to pay my respects to the family for their loss.'

Lara stared hard, her legs threatening to buckle beneath her. She was suddenly aware that Gabriel Devenish, her brother's best friend at university, hadn't recognised her.

Her initial reaction was to feel blessedly relieved, but that was quickly followed by a churning in her guts that made her fear she might faint.

The memory of Gabriel had haunted her for years.

He and Sean had studied for the same degree together. But while the big-hearted Sean had elected to go into charity work after graduating, Gabriel had followed in his rich uncle's footsteps and gone into the more lucrative and some might say cut-throat world of high finance.

Her brother had once told her that he'd heard on the grapevine that his friend had made an absolute fortune since moving to New York, but he'd said it in a way that had implied he almost felt sorry for him.

In any case, from the very first moment that Lara had set eyes on Gabriel, on a blistering-hot summer's day thirteen years ago, when she'd been just sixteen, she had developed the most massive crush on him. She might have been four years younger, and still at school, but that hadn't tempered her feelings. And a foolish impulse that she had lived to regret had once driven her to confess them to him.

Her memory was transported back to that night when Sean had thrown an impromptu party for some friends at the house when their parents were away.

Seeking to bolster her courage, because Gabriel had been there, Lara had drunk a little too much wine and had consequently embarrassed herself. Dancing with him a few hours later when the party was in full swing, delighted by his flirtatious comments and what she'd imagined was an invitational smile, she'd reciprocated by shyly telling him how much she liked him…that she liked him a *lot*, in fact. Then, shutting her eyes, she had moved her face up to his for a kiss.

She still remembered the look of shock on his face and the sensation of hurt that had flooded her when he'd firmly but carefully moved her away, telling her that she was his friend's little sister and that she'd read him wrong…he'd only been teasing her.

Lara practically remembered what he'd said to her word for word. He'd added, *I'm sure there are plenty of boys your own age who would love to go out with you, Lara, but I'm a little too old for you, I fear. Anyway,*

I have my sights set on that tall, slim blonde standing over there. She's one of my tutors and has made no secret of the fact that she likes me.'

Even the false sense of courage that the alcohol had given her hadn't been able to protect Lara from being devastated by Gabriel's rejection.... Yes, devastated, and *humiliated*, too. Over and over again she'd speculated on the reasons why he'd spurned her. Had it really been just because she was younger than him and because she was Sean's 'little sister'? If you cared for a person—*really* cared—then what did it signify that there was a bit of an age difference?

Lara had been left with the conclusion that, apart from the bond of friendship that was between them because she was his best friend's sister, Gabriel didn't care for her at all. Even back then he'd set his sights on much more potentially lucrative opportunities—a prime example being the slim blonde tutor from his university.

Ever since that painful incident at the party Lara's relationships with men had never seemed to progress much beyond friendship, even when she'd wished that they would. The trouble was she no longer trusted herself to read the correct signals as far as the opposite sex were concerned. Also, in spite of Gabriel's rejection, she realised that she still harboured impossibly romantic feelings towards her brother's friend. Had she turned him into a bit of a fantasy figure over the years? A fantasy that no other man could possibly hope to live up to?

He had definitely been a hard man to forget....

Lara's throat was uncomfortably dry, but looking back at him now, she somehow managed to speak.

'It's Gabriel, isn't it? Gabriel Devenish? You were my brother's best friend when he was at university. I'm sorry but my parents aren't here at the moment. They've gone away to the south of France for a break.'

Behind Lara, hating to be ignored, Barney started barking again. Glad of the momentary distraction in order to gather herself mentally, she instantly dropped down to her haunches to stroke his rough wheaten-coloured coat affectionately.

'Hush, Barney, you don't have to make such a fuss.'

'You're Lara? Sean's little sister?'

Lifting her gaze, she fell into Gabriel's mesmerising crystal-blue stare like a diver plunging straight into the sunlit Mediterranean.

With her heart slamming against her ribs, she nodded slowly. 'That's right. Though not so little any more, I'm afraid.'

Rising to her full height again—five feet seven of slim limbs and womanly curves in light blue denims and a fitted white shirt—she was nothing like the plump, awkward teenager she'd been when she was sixteen. It was no surprise that Gabriel hadn't recognised her.

'Well, I'll be…'

He seemed to be genuinely shocked. Lara even detected a faint flush of heat in his chiselled countenance.

'You *have* grown up. Look…'

Tunnelling his long fingers through his thick chestnut hair, he inadvertently drew her attention to his strong, indomitable brow—a brow that was etched with two deeply hewn furrows. It didn't suggest he utilised that devastating smile of his very often these days. Whatever road life had taken him down it hadn't all been plain sailing, she thought. He might be rich, but no matter how much money a person had it didn't protect them from the slings and arrows that life aimed at everyone along the way... No one got off scot-free.

'I only learned of Sean's death yesterday,' Gabriel confessed. 'I saw an article in the newspaper about charity workers that had died of malaria and his name was mentioned. The piece said that he'd recently won a prestigious award for his work. I was stunned to hear that he'd died. I feel bad that I never kept in touch with him after we left university.'

'You took different paths.' Lara shrugged, her smile unsure.

She'd hate Gabriel to think she was criticising him, even though she'd never understood why he'd chosen to go into a profession that, in her view, was about taking rather than giving—a profession that was the polar opposite of Sean's.

'But it's good of you to call round to pay your respects. Mum and Dad will be touched when I tell them. I'm sure you must know they were very fond of you. Anyway, you're probably busy, so I won't keep you.'

Lara fervently willed him to take the cue she'd offered and leave. There was no way she wanted him to think that she was especially pleased to see him again. She was no longer the foolish sixteen-year-old whose crush on him had probably painfully embarrassed him.

But Gabriel sighed and stayed where he was. 'Look...I don't mean to be presumptuous, but is there any chance of a cup of tea? I promise not to take up too much of your time.'

As much as she wished she could come up with a convincing excuse that she was indeed busy, Lara had glimpsed an unexpected look of vulnerability in his eyes and she didn't have the heart to refuse him.

'Why don't you come in?' she invited. 'I was just about to have one myself.'

Feeling relieved, Gabriel followed Lara down the hallway towards what he remembered was a spacious and homely kitchen. As he walked slowly behind the brunette his astonishment that the sometimes shy and bookish teenager had blossomed into such a beauty made him stare at her shapely hourglass figure in wonder.

What her curvaceous body did for a simple pair of jeans and plain white shirt should be committed to art or poetry, he mused. Even though he wasn't remotely artistic or poetic himself, it certainly didn't mean he didn't appreciate the more aesthetically pleasing things in life—which was why he'd selected a New York apartment that had a stunning view of the Metropolitan Museum of Art.

Every now and then, when he found the time, he'd visit to remind himself that money wasn't the only thing in life worth appreciating. Yes, it gave a person a lot more options if he had it, but it didn't buy happiness. God knew he'd learned that to his cost over the years.... The contemplation of beauty and art 'soothed the troubled soul', as one wise guide at the museum had put it to him once, and although he would never dream of sharing such a view with any of his colleagues, Gabriel had agreed. That was why he admired the artists who created it.

But his admiration of Lara's beauty was set aside as he entered the kitchen. It was indeed as homely as he remembered. And the old-fashioned stand-alone fixtures and fittings, including the 1930s pillarbox-red

AGA, straight away transported him right back to when he and Sean had been young.

He recalled with fondness the countless delicious meals Peggy Bradley had made for them—in particular during that seemingly 'endless' summer when he and Sean, in between revising for their exams, had laughed and joked together, listened to the music of their favourite bands, mercilessly teased Lara and generally enjoyed being young and free of care, not burdened with responsibility as so many of the adults that they'd known had seemed to be. It had been easy to fantasise then that that those halcyon days would last for ever....

Gabriel's senses were suddenly awash in a sea of poignant and heartfelt memory. As if to compound his feelings, he saw that the cream dresser was full of engaging family pictures, and taking pride of place was an eye-catching photograph of Sean as he must have looked before he died. His mischievous brown eyes were full of laughter and his wide smile highlighted the chipped front tooth that Gabriel had accidentally broken when he'd too zealously bowled a cricket ball in the garden for him to bat. He had been the closest friend that Gabriel had ever had, and even though he hadn't kept in touch with him it cut him to the quick to think that he was no longer here....

'Everything looks just the same,' he remarked huskily, reaching his hand up to loosen the shirt collar that suddenly felt constricting.

'Mum and Dad aren't great lovers of change. They're old-fashioned like that.' Lara smiled fondly. 'Not to mention sentimental. They've become even more so since losing Sean.' Her smile vanished and, clearly needing a moment, she turned towards the sink to fill the kettle.

'It must have been a terrible shock to you all to receive the news that he'd died,' Gabriel murmured sympathetically.

'It was. One minute we were talking to him on Skype, hearing all about the events of his day, and the next...' Sadly shaking her head, Lara turned off the tap that had been gushing water into the kettle then moved across to the generous granite worktop to plug it into a socket to boil. 'How do you like your tea?' she asked, tucking some of her glossy dark hair behind her ear as she turned back.

'Don't you remember?' Gabriel teased, recalling with pleasure the numerous cups of tea an eager-to-please young Lara had made him whenever he'd stayed over or visited Sean. 'I used to tell you that, next to your mum, you made the best cup of tea in the world.'

'You did, didn't you?' Her generous mouth curved with pleasure. 'Okay, then, I'll see if I can remember how you like it. Don't tell me—just let me have a go. Pull up a chair and make yourself comfortable.'

He didn't need to be asked twice. This house was the only place he'd ever known that really felt like home, with everything that that word represented.

Jaded and tired from the demands and rigours of inhabiting the soulless world of high finance for what had probably been too many years to stay wholly sane, Gabriel had a secret yearning for some simplicity and comfort in his life. He was frankly weary of the kind of comfort epitomised by the opulent living of a lot of bankers in New York, although he himself had embraced it, thinking it was his 'due' for working so hard and making others as rich as he was.

He hadn't fully explored the realisation, but he was longing for the kind of comfort that might be attained by being amongst people who were authentic, with no hidden agendas and the ability simply to be themselves. In short, people who were naturally *good* rather than unscrupulously self-seeking.

And even as he had the thought his mind went straight away to Lara's parents. They had welcomed him into their home without any judgement or expectation when their son had befriended him, and had even expressed their sadness that he'd been raised by a wealthy but often absent uncle who more often than not had left him in the care of a hired nanny. They were appalled that Gabriel had never known the joys of growing up in a 'real' family as Sean had.

'Would you like some toast and marmalade with your cuppa?'

'Sorry...what did you say?' Blinking up into the melting chocolate-brown eyes of the lovely brunette who was suddenly standing in front of him, for a surreal moment Gabriel honestly forgot who or where he was because she was so enchanting.

Her brow puckering, Lara seemed taken aback that he hadn't heard her the first time. *Perhaps she didn't know how mesmerising she was?* He shrugged. He doubted it. He hadn't met a beautiful woman yet who wasn't intimately aware of her own appeal. Beauty was a very desirable cachet in the avaricious world that he inhabited—not to mention an *asset*. In his opinion every attractive woman who aimed for the top in his profession had no compunction in using such an advantage to the max.

'I just asked if you'd like some toast and marmalade with your tea….'

'Just tea will do thanks. Then, if you've got the time, I'd like you to sit down and talk to me. We've got quite a bit of catching up to do. It's been years since we've seen each other, Lara, and as well as talking about Sean I'd like to hear what you've been doing with yourself.'

'Okay.' She chewed down on her lip, as if taken aback by the invitation. 'But didn't you say you'd just flown back from New York? Don't you need to at least relax and unwind for a little while after your flight?'

Gabriel couldn't help but smile. It seemed that the once self-conscious and unsure teenager had inherited some of her mother's endearing natural ability to think of others' needs first. It wasn't something he often came across in his world—if *ever*—and he had to admit it was appealing. But he could just imagine the response of his more cynical male colleagues should they meet Lara and be exposed to her kind disposition for very long. They'd wonder if she was 'for real'.

'I assure you that right now I don't need to do anything else other than be here with you, Lara.'

If ever a man's statement had sounded more seductive and appealing then Lara hadn't heard one. And the huskily low-pitched velvet cadence of Gabriel's deeply arresting voice couldn't help but render the words even more provocative. Her insides felt as though they'd suddenly been heated by a fiercely burning erotic flame. Could it be that her teenage fascination for this man hadn't died with his rejection of her at that party, but instead had been quietly simmering inside all these years?

The realisation was akin to standing on a crumbling cliff edge and frantically trying to maintain her balance. It had been thirteen long years since she'd seen this man. She knew nothing about his life now, or what had transpired in the years since they'd last met, and she was pretty certain that if he had any interest in her at all at this moment it was only because of his past association with her family.

For all Lara knew, the man could be happily married to a stunningly perfect model wife in New York— the kind epitomised by the glossy magazines—with a brood of pretty blue-eyed offspring to boot. Her stomach helplessly churned at the thought.

'All right, then. I'll make us some tea and then we'll catch up. Just don't expect any tales of adventure or excitement. I live a very quiet and ordinary life that's probably miles away from how you live yours.'

Giving him a faintly wry smile, she moved back across the kitchen to the granite worktop and hurriedly arranged the teapot and matching china cups and saucers on a tray. But her hands were visibly trembling as she poured hot water onto the tea leaves, and her heart was pounding as though it would never be at ease or calm again....

They moved into the living room to drink their tea, and Lara opened the generous-sized patio doors that led out onto the garden so that they might enjoy the sunshine. She also didn't want to miss the opportunity of hearing the birds sing. That was one of the reasons why early morning had always been her favourite time of the day.

'You've made it just how I like it,' her handsome visitor announced, taking a sip of his tea as he lowered his long-limbed frame down into one of the comfortable Chesterfield armchairs. 'You've got a good memory.'

'Thanks.'

Suddenly self-conscious, Lara sat down in the chair opposite him and stirred own tea. She'd never been able to drink the beverage without at least one sugar. *She'd bet that Gabriel never touched the stuff.* Even though he'd acquired a couple of lines on his forehead over the years, his lean, toned physique radiated the vim and vigour of a seasoned athlete rather than someone who spent his days immersed in making eye-popping deals on Wall Street.

The thought prompted a question. 'You said you'd just come back from New York? Is this a flying visit or are you going to stay for a while?'

A definitely guarded expression stole into his mesmerising blue eyes and his lean jaw clenched a little. Leaning forward, he placed his cup and saucer down onto the walnut coffee table arranged between them.

'I'm not sure. Right now I've no idea how long I'll stay. I've come back to deal with some legalities regarding my uncle's estate, to tell you the truth. He died a few weeks ago and I'm his sole beneficiary.'

'Oh, Gabriel, I'm so sorry...about your uncle dying, I mean. Did you come back for the funeral?'

'I did. Anyway, I have a meeting with his solicitor tomorrow.'

He shook his head, as though the matter pained rather than gratified him. But then why should he be pleased by the fact that his only family member had died? Lara reasoned. Even if he had bequeathed him everything he owned? If the scant details that she knew about Gabriel's upbringing by his uncle were right, then surely he would have preferred to have the man's love and affection, not to mention caring support, when he was a boy, rather than be left all his worldly goods when he died? Did he even *need* them when he was purported to be so wealthy in his own right?

'Did you see your uncle much over the years after you left to go to New York?'

'No, I didn't. We weren't close. He adopted me when my mother—his sister—decided she wasn't cut out to be a mother after all…that she wanted her freedom above all else. At least he was decent enough to do that, I suppose.'

'What about your father?' Lara frowned. 'What happened to him?'

In answer Gabriel's brow creased in a formidable scowl. 'Your guess is as good as mine. My mother put him down as "unknown" on my birth certificate.'

'How sad.' The comment was out before she could check it.

'Why? I grew up in an impressive home in a very desirable area and I wanted for nothing. What's sad about that?'

'It's sad that you never knew your real father, or had a relationship with him, and it's sad that you weren't close to the uncle who adopted you—that's all I meant.'

'Well, don't give it another thought. In the circles I move in I'm considered to be a great success, and everything I've achieved I've accomplished on my own. I wasn't held back by the fact that I wasn't close to my family or they to me. End of story.'

But Lara guessed that was *far* from the end. She was pretty certain that anyone who'd been abandoned by their mother as a child must have a river of pain and anger flowing through them that couldn't help but affect their sense of self-esteem and self-worth. But she sensed, too, that now wasn't the time to try and press Gabriel into telling her more. He'd come to pay his respects to the family for Sean, not to be grilled by his friend's sister about his less than idyllic upbringing.

'Anyway, I'd like to hear about what you've been up to since we last met.' Deftly, he changed the subject. 'What do you do for a living? If I remember rightly, you were either going to be a vet or a politician. We had some passionate discussions, you, me and Sean, about setting the world to rights, didn't we?'

His comment made Lara burn with embarrassment as she remembered their often heated and animated discussions. Especially when she recalled that her views had always been the most passionate and vehement. But when you were sixteen you thought you knew everything. You could even fool yourself into believing that a more experienced older man could seriously fall for you, when, in truth, he was only flirting with you because he could....

'Well, I didn't become a vet *or* a politician,' she said. 'Being responsible for setting the world to rights was too tall an order, so I became a librarian instead.'

'Well, well, well...a librarian?' Gabriel's expression was wry. 'I know you loved books, but I always thought you were far too passionate to squirrel yourself away in some dusty hall, lending them out to the great unwashed public!'

'In case you hadn't noticed, we're not living in the Dickensian era.'

Lara couldn't help but bristle at his mocking tone, but at the same time she couldn't help registering the disturbing fact that he'd called her 'passionate'. Had he always thought that about her? The thought made her heart race even as she reminded herself that he'd once painfully rejected her.

'Amongst other things, I issue books in a state-of-the-art college library with every bit of modern technology you can imagine at my disposal. If you think I chose a "safe" option in becoming a librarian, instead of a vet or a politician, then I can assure you that dealing every day with the demands of diverse and sometimes tricky students is no walk in the park.'

'But you love it?' Lifting a dark eyebrow, Gabriel smiled. 'I'm glad that you found a career you enjoy, Lara. And, just for the record, I still think you're passionate. I'm sure you would be whatever you decided to do in life. You can't help your nature.'

CHAPTER TWO

'AND WHAT ABOUT YOU, GABRIEL?' Lara asked, feeling suddenly hot again, because she seemed to be the focus of attention and she would much prefer to learn more about him. 'What line of work are you in these days? Are you still involved in finance?'

The smile Gabriel returned was faintly rueful. 'Yes, I am.'

'What exactly do you do? I mean, do you have a job title?'

In answer he rose to his feet, and it was clear to Lara that her questions were unsettling him.

'I'm a CRO on Wall Street—and, before you ask, that stands for Chief Risk Officer. I deal with analysing risk-and-reward formulas in financial businesses and banks.'

'Oh.' She raised her shoulders in a shrug, feeling none the wiser with the explanation. 'It sounds complicated.'

'Does it?' A visible muscle flinched at the side of his carved cheekbone. 'At any rate, I'd advise you not to lose any sleep trying to figure it out.'

'Meaning you don't think I'm intelligent enough to understand?'

'You always did take umbrage when you thought I

was being mocking, didn't you? Perhaps you should try not to take things so personally.'

As Lara mulled over the comment, to try and ascertain exactly what he meant, Gabriel moved across to where she sat, leaned down and gathered her hands in his. Then he silently pulled her to her feet.

There wasn't an adequate description for the huge wave of both panic and pleasure that suddenly engulfed her…except maybe abject disbelief that it was happening. Over the years, she had fantasised many times about what it might be like if Gabriel ever touched her or held her close as if he meant it, and while her heart sang to have him near she couldn't help but remember the time when he'd so purposefully moved her away from him and told her he could never be for her. But even that agonising memory couldn't stop her from thinking that being close to him like this felt so—so *right*.

Then she realised that his brilliant blue gaze was examining her with a searching intensity that couldn't help but make her apprehensive.

'Tell me about Sean,' he commanded quietly, his tone almost reverent, as though even uttering his friend's name out loud distressed him.

Relieved that it wasn't anything she'd inadvertently done or said that had made him study her so intently, Lara took a nervous swallow. It still upset her terribly to talk about Sean and remember afresh that he had died. The thought was akin to sharpened cold steel being plunged into her heart.

'What do you want to know?'

Gabriel didn't release her and she found she was in no hurry to be free. His hands were large and warm and they made her feel strangely secure, made her ache for the kind of loving, sensual protection that only a man like him could provide. She was suddenly aware of a small vein throbbing in his forehead.

'Why—*how* did he contract malaria?' he enquired huskily. 'Don't volunteers have to have some kind of protection before going out into these godforsaken places?'

'Of course they do.' Lara was taken aback by the underlying rage she heard in his voice…touched that he still felt so strongly about Sean after all these years.

She was angry, too, that the brother she'd loved so dearly had been ripped from her so suddenly and without warning, and the wounds of that loss were so great she feared they might never heal. Yet she wouldn't run away from grief, no matter how hard it hurt. She'd made a vow to face it head-on and not wound her heart further by denying how she felt. Something told her that it would be disrespectful to Sean if she did. But still, she utterly sympathised with Gabriel's confusion and pain.

'He had all the necessary jabs and medical examinations before he went over there,' she said softly, 'but malaria is caused by a mosquito bite from an infected mosquito, as I'm sure you probably know. Shortly after his death, a tear in the netting over his bed was discovered. Unfortunately the charity was always short of the money to be able to replace the old ones when they were no longer any good.'

'So he was given a faulty mosquito net?' His tone disparaging, Gabriel abruptly dropped Lara's hands and stepped away.

Feeling both bereft of his touch and chilled by the

memory of how Sean had died, she crossed her arms over her cotton shirt and nodded sadly. 'It seems so.'

As if he didn't know what to do with his rage to contain it, he strode over to the other side of the room to stare blindly out at the sunlit garden. Suddenly he spun round again to face her. 'How could Sean have been such an idiot?' he asked angrily.

'What?' The brutal question had the same effect on Lara as if Gabriel had slapped her hard across the face.

'I mean, why didn't he think of the consequences of being so careless about his own welfare? Probably because he'd never dream of putting himself first— and that was the problem. Why else would he accept a faulty net and risk being bitten? Even if he hadn't realised it wasn't intact. He should have checked. But he was always too busy thinking about others, wasn't he? No wonder he went into charity work. What a waste *that* turned out to be.'

His blue eyes glittered with fury and then, seconds later, looked utterly *desolate*.

'He was a genius at maths and science. He could have gone into any investment bank or financial concern and gone straight to the top. If it was so important to him to support worthy causes he could have done so from the safety of his office, using as much of his money as he wanted, without putting himself in the eye of the damn storm! It's a dog-eat-dog world out there—a world where it's every man for himself— and if you don't make yourself number one then you're dead in the water.'

As Gabriel angrily scraped his fingers through his hair it was clear that it was near impossible for him to contain his growing frustration.

'God knows I told him that enough times. You'd think he would have had the common sense to take it on board.'

Taking a deep breath in, Lara slowly breathed out again. Her anxious heartbeat started to ease and return to a calmer rhythm. Gabriel hadn't been being cruel when he'd asked how Sean could have been such an idiot—he was merely angry and frustrated at the senseless waste of his friend's life. As they *all* were.

'My brother was a good man—as I'm sure you know, Gabriel. And he was happy doing the work he'd chosen, helping others less fortunate than he was. It simply wasn't in his nature to put himself first. I don't know about you, but that's the way I want to remember him. Happy and fulfilled and enjoying his life. I know that if he were still here he'd want you to be happy and fulfilled and enjoying your life, too. *Are* you?'

Her question hung suspended in the air like the sword of Damocles. Gabriel was staring at her as though transfixed, but then he rubbed his hand round his jaw in a bid to stir himself from the seeming trance he'd fallen into and shrugged.

'In my view, being happy is given too much credence in this world. A far better goal is to aim to be successful. If you're successful then that's fulfilling. That at least gives you choices in life. Anyway...'

Moving back to his chair, he lifted his cup of tea to his lips and took a long draught. Then he put the cup and saucer back down and gave Lara a haunting smile that was part regret, part anguish.

'I'm sorry if I upset you with my rant about Sean. But he was a good friend to me—probably the best friend I've ever had. I only wish I'd realised it sooner. I should have stayed in touch with him—but it's too late now, isn't it? It's an absolute crime and a travesty that he was taken from us so soon. Please convey my heart-felt condolences to your parents, won't you? I'm sorry they aren't here for me to speak to personally. At any rate, I think it's probably about time I went.'

The thought that he was leaving and that she might never see him again hit Lara like a thunderbolt.

Before she was sufficiently recovered from the shock to think it through properly, she blurted out, 'Must you go? If you stay for a while we can have lunch together. You can even come for a walk with me and Barney first, if you like? A walk is the perfect remedy to blow the cobwebs away and clear your head. We've got woods at the back of the house, remember? I wish you'd seen them when the primroses were out in the spring—they were a picture.'

It was at that very moment that Gabriel knew he couldn't walk away from this woman as easily as he wanted to—as easily as he *should* walk away. Because he knew if he stayed he would only hurt her. The sav-age hunger and need that he had buried inside for so long—and from time to time had sought to assuage with pretty bodies who only saw him as a 'golden ticket' to the lavish and expensive lifestyle they craved—would only end up consuming the innocent Lara and filling her with the most bitter regret for issuing that invita-tion to stay a while.

But Gabriel knew already that he couldn't resist ac-cepting it. And who could blame him for seeking sanc-tuary in her fresh and innocent company for a little while longer?

'All right, then. I'll stay…at least for lunch and a walk with Barney.'

'That's great. But you *do* realise I have an ulterior motive for asking?'

She smiled, and for the first time Gabriel noticed the two engaging and rather sexy dimples in her cheeks. But her words suddenly made him stiffen. He wasn't ready for his illusions about her—if illusions were what they were—to be shattered so soon.

'What motive would that be?' he asked warily.

She lifted her slender shoulders, then dropped them again. 'It's just that I've been a bit lonely here on my own, surrounded by memories of my brother. It would be nice to have some company for a change to help take my mind off things…. That's all I meant.'

Feeling ridiculously pleased at the admission, Gabriel relaxed. 'Then far be it from me to deny you the one thing I can give you today. Shall we go for that walk now? The sun is shining and it's a beautiful day. It would be a shame to waste it staying indoors.'

'I agree.' Lifting her long dark hair off her shoulders and dropping it down again behind her back, Lara moved gracefully across to the door. 'I'll just go and get my walking boots on—the terrain in the woods is quite rough and uneven in places. Will you be okay walking in those?' Her glance was doubtful as she surveyed the ebony Italian loafers that he wore. 'They look pretty chic and expensive.'

'I would have brought something more suitable to change into if I'd known you were going to entice me into the woods with you,' he remarked drolly, and his lips split into a grin when she blushed vividly.

'Don't kid yourself I'd even dream of such a thing.
For one thing, I wouldn't know how.'

Beneath his immaculate white shirt Gabriel's heart
started to pound disturbingly. More than that, a profoundly arousing heat invaded his blood.

'Now, there's a challenge if ever I heard one...' he
commented huskily.

'I didn't mean it as a challenge. I was only— Oh,
never mind. I'll go and get my boots on.'

Clearly flustered, Lara hurriedly left the room, and
straight away Gabriel missed her presence and longed
for her to return.

He was being introduced to a completely different world
from the one he was used to inhabiting—a world that
he realised he'd been missing for far too long.

Walking through the woods with the beauty he had
once known as 'Sean's little sister' by his side was delightful. She laughed often and unselfconsciously—a
huskily engaging sound that made all the hairs stand up
on the back of his neck. And every now and then a waft
of the delightful perfume she wore, which smelled like
a bouquet of wild flowers, deluged Gabriel's senses and
hit him in the gut. Coupled with the earthy, resinous
scents that abounded in the woods, it made for a sensual experience bar none—a million miles away from
the tense, charged atmosphere of Wall Street that was
his usual daily experience.

'I'm going to take Barney's lead off now. This is his
favourite neck of the woods. We know it well and I like
to let him have a run.'

Gifting Gabriel with another sunny smile, Lara
stooped to free the excited terrier from his leash and

he bounded away through the thicket of dense undergrowth and trees like a whippet, joyously barking.

'He's not the brightest chicken in the coop,' she commented affectionately. 'He's a natural hunter, but the trouble is he announces his arrival so that his prey can get away before he reaches it!'

Shaking her head in amusement, she laughed again, and Gabriel couldn't help but smile with pleasure. Driven by sheer instinct—for once letting his heart rule his head—he found himself drawing closer and reaching for her hand. The hotly fierce tingle that shot through his body when he touched her was like being glanced by lightning and almost made him stumble. The startled look Lara gave him in return indicated that she'd felt the electrifying sensation, too.

'I'd forgotten how funny you are,' he confessed. 'And that you have the most beautiful eyes. They glisten like jewels when you laugh.' It didn't come naturally to him to compliment a woman and mean it, but he meant this particular one with every fibre of his being.

'Thank you.'

Carefully she disengaged her hand from his, and the becoming flush on Lara's cheeks told Gabriel that he'd been right about her being disturbed by the shock of electricity that had arced between them.

'You're blushing,' he teased.

'If I am it's because I'm not used to receiving such effusive compliments.'

'Not even from the man in your life?'

He experienced no remorse whatsoever for shamelessly fishing. But Lara's expression looked troubled now, and the light in her eyes dimmed a little.

'There isn't a man in my life—at least not at the moment.'

Gabriel couldn't deny he was relieved to hear it, although he wasn't ready to explore *why* right then.

'You mean to say that there potentially *might* be someone? Someone you perhaps have your eye on?'

'No. I don't mean that at all.' She didn't bother to try and disguise her annoyance that he should quiz her on the subject.

'What about you?' she asked, turning the tables. 'Is there anyone significant in *your* life? For all I know you might even be married by now.'

'I'm not—married, I mean. And neither am I in a serious relationship. I'm married to my work, Lara. I know that sounds extremely dull and boring but it's true. However, that's not to say I lack the company of a pretty woman when I want it.'

'You mean you like to play the field? I suppose that's why there's no one serious in your life, then.'

She sighed. But whether that sigh signified disapproval or disappointment Gabriel couldn't guess.

Staring at the dense shroud of trees and bushes that her lively pet terrier had disappeared into, she suddenly called out, 'Barney! Here, boy! Come on back, now.'

When the dog didn't immediately appear, Lara turned her gaze back to Gabriel.

'I worry when he suddenly goes quiet,' she admitted, 'I'd better go and see where he's got to. He might have got stuck down a rabbit hole or something. It's happened before. Why don't you wait here for me? You've already got your posh shoes all muddy, and the ground on the other side of those trees and bushes is invariably quite boggy. Hopefully I won't be too long.'

'I don't give a damn about my shoes, and I haven't left my jacket back at the house and rolled up my shirt-sleeves for nothing. I'm not concerned about getting dirty. I'll come and help you find the dog.'

'His name's Barney!'

Again Lara looked affronted, and again Gabriel couldn't resist goading her.

'Who's he named after? One of your ex-boyfriends?'

'He's my parents' dog, not mine, you ninny.'

'You always used to call me that. You might be surprised to know I found it quite endearing.'

'Now, that I *don't* believe. My perception was that it irritated you. I was the pesky sixteen-year-old sister of your friend, remember? You didn't take me at all seriously. You put up with me out of politeness to Sean and my parents, I'm sure.'

'That's not true.' Gabriel frowned, perturbed that Lara had believed that.

'Come on, then.' As if intuiting his disturbance, she gave him a cheery smile. 'Let's go and find Barney.'

As he squelched through the dense and muddied undergrowth in his thousand-dollar Italian loafers, with the damp leaves of bushes and thickets brushing against his immaculate white shirt, occasionally stumbling when he lost his balance, Gabriel had to smile at the ludicrous image he must present. His colleagues on Wall Street would have a field day if they could see him.

Strangely enough, that made him smile even more. In truth, he wasn't predisposed to be glum or morose. He honestly thought that he had the best of it. How could he *not* when he was following behind the long-legged beauty in tight jeans in front of him?

Lara was negotiating the uneven muddy trail through

the woods like a latter-day female Indiana Jones, hardly pausing for breath and calling out 'Barney!' every now and then with renewed gusto. Gabriel knew himself to be a fit man who welcomed a challenge—be it mental or physical—but his companion's agility and stamina had to be seen to be believed.

Suddenly coming to a halt, and with frustration and apprehension in her voice, Lara shouted, '*Barney!* This isn't funny. What do you think you're playing at, you naughty boy?'

'Sounds like you're expecting him to reply.'

'Ha-ha, very funny…*not.*'

This time Gabriel was treated to an irritated glare which, thankfully, he didn't take seriously—not when he guessed that Lara would be utterly distraught if they couldn't find the dog. It made him want to make more of a concerted effort to help her.

'Barney!' he yelled, striding towards an even denser section of the woods that they hadn't yet explored, at that point not giving a fig that his shoes were now more or less ruined by the rough, muddy terrain.

Was that a glimpse of a dark sandy-coloured coat he'd just spied through the trees? He squinted searchingly. Gabriel would bet his bottom dollar that it was.

'Barney! Here, boy!' he called again, moving more deeply into the shrouded area in front of him.

He hadn't gone very far when he saw the terrier's wriggling rear-end pointed upwards towards the sheltering canopy of leaves. The dog was furiously digging in the earth as though intent on finding treasure.

'I've found him!' he called out to Lara, spinning round only to find her hurrying towards him. Her white shirt was splattered with mud, as his was, her long dark hair was engagingly dishevelled, and her pretty face was visibly flushed pink with the heat of her exertions.

'Thank God!' she exclaimed as she flew past Gabriel to reach her adored family pet, dropping down onto her knees on the rough woodland floor.

She didn't seem to care that she might potentially hurt herself or ruin her clothes.

'Barney, you're a very naughty boy,' she scolded fondly, lifting the animal away from his enthusiastic digging and hugging him to her chest, uncaring that the terrier had made her white shirt even muddier.

Crazy as it was, Gabriel couldn't help but *envy* the small hound. He wouldn't mind his once spotless tailored shirt getting even dirtier if Lara held him to her fulsome breasts like that.

'He was probably digging for rabbits.' She grinned up at him, her dark eyes shining. 'He can't help himself.' Turning back to the dog, she crooned, 'You're a natural-born hunter, aren't you, baby?'

Then, before Gabriel could take command of his besieged senses and help her, she gracefully rose to her feet and slipped the leash back on the terrier's collar.

'I don't know about you, but I'm suddenly starving. Let's get back and I'll fix us some lunch.'

Starving didn't come close to describing Gabriel's appetite right then—and it wasn't food that he hungered for. His best friend's little sister was seriously challenging his libido and winning. Of all the things he might have envisaged happening on this trip to the UK, it wasn't that.

Just what the hell he was going to do about it he didn't rightly know. But to seriously consider bedding the shapely brunette and risk sullying his once good relationship with her and her family almost didn't bear thinking about.

'I want you to take off that shirt when we get home,' Lara instructed as she airily swept past him with Barney.

'What?'

Coming to a sudden halt, she turned to flourish at him a cheeky grin that would've shamed a mischievous schoolgirl.

'Don't worry—it's not because I have designs on your body or anything. You're quite safe. I was just going to put it in the washing machine. You can borrow one of my dad's shirts in the meantime. He's about the same build and height as you, although of course not quite as—not quite as...'

As her big brown eyes swept over him, and she clearly struggled to finish the sentence, Gabriel once again couldn't resist being provocative.

'Fit?' he suggested, smiling.

'You know that saying? It should be "Vanity, thy name is *Man*—not Woman".'

Crossing his arms over his shirtfront, Gabriel mockingly raised an eyebrow. 'That quote is from Hamlet, and it's, "*Frailty*, thy name is woman"—*not* vanity. Just thought you'd like to know that for future reference.'

His pretty companion tossed her head and spun away, striding through the undergrowth again with Barney yapping happily beside her—but not before Gabriel saw her look daggers at him, as if she'd like to abandon him in the middle of those dank, dark woods and leave him there.

Lara honestly didn't know where she was finding the courage to deal with the disturbingly charismatic pres-

ence that was Gabriel. And neither had she fully dealt
with the shock of him turning up out of the blue like
that at her parents' door.

As time had gone on, her day had grown more challenging. When they'd been chatting in the living room
earlier and Gabriel had drawn her up from her chair
to ask about Sean she'd really believed she might faint
from the sheer dizzying pleasure of the contact—not to
mention the mesmerisingly intense glance he'd given
her. His brilliant blue eyes had stared back into hers as
though wanting to see into her very soul…as though
even that wouldn't be enough for him to find what he
was searching for.

She'd seen so many things in that seemingly endless
glance to take her breath away, but rage and hunger—
for what, she didn't know—had been predominant.

The second time he'd touched her, catching hold
of her hand in the woods and smiling down at her, as
though her company genuinely gave him pleasure, the
sizzling jolt of electricity Lara had experienced when
he put his hand round hers had left her feeling dizzy
and confused. Such an extreme reaction to a simple
friendly touch didn't bode well for her peace of mind
when the time came for her to say goodbye to Gabriel
again. And this time she didn't doubt his departure
would be for good.

He would go back to his high-octane life on Wall
Street and she would return to her much more simple
and ordinary routine as a college librarian. Except that
would be no consolation for watching her brother's one-
time charismatic best friend walk out of her life for a
second time….

On their return from the woods they stood in the

porch at the back of the house as Lara schooled Barney to wait while she and Gabriel removed their muddy footwear. Seeing that her companion's black loafers were liberally weighed down and caked in once-oozing but now dried sludge, she let out a groan.

'Oh, why, oh, why did they have to be *suede*?' she asked, sincerely regretful that because of her Gabriel had ruined what was an undoubtedly expensive pair of shoes.

She could just imagine Sean shaking his head and saying, *Not one of your best ideas, sis—taking Gabe on a woodland walk when he was wearing classy Italian loafers. What on earth were you thinking?*

It took her aback to remember that he'd always referred to his friend as Gabe, not Gabriel. Lara had never been bold enough to do the same. Aside from that, Sean would have been right to wonder what she was thinking about. The trouble was her wonderful brother hadn't realised that Lara never *had* been able to think clearly round Gabriel.

'I should have lent you my dad's walking boots,' she reflected ruefully.

'What size is he?'

'He's a nine.'

Grimacing as he stood up in the generous-sized utility room that his impressive physique had made appear suddenly small, Gabriel emitted a playful sigh. 'Wouldn't have been any good, I'm afraid. I'm a size twelve.'

Having removed her own boots, Lara rose to join him. 'In any case, I think your lovely shoes are completely ruined. Were they very expensive?' She flushed as she privately wondered how she could possibly find the money to replace them if they'd been even half as expensive as she guessed they had. God knew a college librarian didn't earn a fortune....

'If I told you, you'd probably read me the riot act for being so vain and wasteful. Forget about it. The damn shoes don't matter. Anyway, I've got a spare pair in the car.'

'You've got a spare pair in the car? Why didn't you tell me?'

His arresting gaze made him look to be carefully considering the question. 'I didn't think about it. Besides, it's no big deal. Now, if you'll go and get me that shirt you promised, I'll get out of this one and give it to you to put in the washing machine.'

He was already starting to unbutton the stained shirt as he spoke, and Lara suddenly panicked at the thought of seeing him standing there bare-chested.

'Okay...won't be a tick,' she murmured, hurriedly turning towards the door that led out into the hall.

Her senses were already bombarded by Gabriel's presence alone—how was she supposed to handle being presented with the arresting beauty of his naked male chest and act as though she were unaffected?

CHAPTER THREE

FOR A MAN WHO LIKED to be in command of situations, Gabriel found himself to be uncharacteristically all at sea in his old friend's home with Lara. Being in that house again, and recalling some of the happiest memories he had ever known, made him yearn to replicate the feelings they evoked—the predominant one being a sense of belonging.

He hadn't experienced that reassuring sense of being welcomed, being regarded without judgement or conditions being attached, since he'd left the UK all those years ago. God knew, the pressurised career he'd chosen wasn't likely to engender anything *close* to that feeling amongst the single-minded and driven individuals he worked with. The phrase about them probably selling their own grandmothers if it made a profit often sprang to Gabriel's mind.

From time to time it alarmed him to realise he was becoming equally mercenary, and he wasn't proud of the fact. But in truth, like all addictions, it was hellishly hard to give up—and making money was definitely his drug of choice. Yet it was strange that he wasn't exactly overjoyed at being bequeathed his uncle's substantial residence, plus all his possessions and a generous monetary legacy.

All attending the man's funeral had done for Gabriel was to remind him of the sense of abandonment and excoriating pain he'd lived with since he was a child and his mother had left, leaving him with a man who—although related to him by blood—had been as distant as the Milky Way and even *less* accessible.

And now, as well as the unwanted complication of having to deal with his uncle's legacy, there was the totally unexpected dilemma of *Lara*. Just knowing that she was in the homely kitchen right now, preparing their lunch, shouldn't give him the inordinate amount of pleasure that it did, but along with an undeniable sense of contentment that *was* how it made him feel. That in itself was unusual, because he hadn't met a woman yet he trusted enough to relax with—except perhaps Peggy Bradley, Lara's mother.

Occupying Lara's father's comfortable wing-backed chair in the living room, Gabriel knew his eyelids were drifting closed, but made no attempt to check their descent. Outside, the beneficent sun was shining and its soporific rays beamed in on him through the opened patio doors and inevitably made him feel sleepy.

On the scented summer air a distant melody floated by, teasing at the memory of a small gathering Sean had once spontaneously thrown at the house.... Lara in a long magenta-and-green dress, dancing for all she was worth, throwing her arms wide as if to embrace all that the world had to offer and drawing his eye more than once because she looked so pretty and so free....

'Gabriel? Sorry to wake you, but lunch is ready. I thought we'd sit out in the garden and eat?'

Hearing the velvet-toned voice of the woman he'd been thinking about, and unsure whether he was still in the throes of his dream or not, Gabriel opened his eyes. His startled gaze was straight away captured by the heart-shaped face that had once been so familiar to him.

Now the innocent young girl that he remembered from his youth had turned into a woman who made him catch his breath and made his blood turn molten simply by looking at her. Devoid of any artifice or make-up, her skin was as fresh and clear as the petals of the creamiest rose, and her lips… Her lush lips were the shape and kind that would draw any man's attention and make him long to know what they would feel like beneath his own if he were lucky enough to kiss them.

Straightening in the chair, he murmured, 'I was dreaming about you….' Playing for time in order to marshal his thoughts, he let a helpless smile tug at the edges of his mouth. 'Yes, I was dreaming about you at a party Sean had once. You were just sixteen and you were dancing like some ethereal wild child to a Jimi Hendrix track. You looked so free and pretty. I remember thinking you would have fitted right into the era of peace and love in the sixties.'

Lara's dark brows furrowed as though the reference displeased her. Clearly that particular recollection from the past didn't fill her with the same wistful pleasure as it did Gabriel.

'Sixteen was a horrible age for me. I was always so self-conscious and shy, and I sometimes said stupid things I didn't mean and came to regret. I said something *very* stupid that night at the party.'

'Did you? Well, you should put it behind you and forget about it. For goodness' sake that was *years* ago, sweetheart, and if my recollections are right I seem to remember that there was plenty of alcohol doing the rounds that night—no doubt that was partly to blame. Besides, we can all say stupid things sometimes. If you can't be stupid when you're sixteen, then when *can* you? Anyway, I was actually quite envious of you that night.'

'Were you? Why?'

'Because you looked so carefree. To me you represented a freedom that I longed for—the kind of freedom that no amount of money could buy me.'

Now it was *his* turn to feel self-conscious and awkward. Gabriel had never revealed anything quite so personal about how he felt to anyone before. Like many young men, the programming that he'd absorbed from an early age had taught him that expressing emotion was akin to revealing a weakness, and right then he kicked it strongly into touch.

Pushing out of his chair, he moved across the room to glance out at the sunlit garden again. Immediately he noticed that the wrought iron picnic table with its matching green umbrella was laid for lunch. It was just the diversion he needed. Too much introspection was liable to make him irritable. He was already regretting being quite so frank with Lara.

'Were you saying something about us eating outside?'

'Yes. Lunch is ready. Why don't you go and make yourself comfortable and I'll bring it out?'

Lara couldn't get Gabriel's remarks about how she had looked at Sean's party out of her mind. At no point had he given any indication that he remembered spurning her—first when she had lifted her face up to his for a kiss and then by tactlessly suggesting there must be boys her own age who were interested in her and telling her he had his sights set on the slim blonde who was his tutor.

He hadn't even taken the bait when Lara had mentioned that she'd said something stupid that night that she regretted. Had her flirtation with him been so insignificant to him that he didn't even remember it? The fact that he'd said he'd been dreaming about her with what sounded like genuine admiration seemed too unreal for words. But, however seductive it sounded, Lara would remain on her guard. She wouldn't let the immature behaviour of her past rule her present by repeating it.

But she also couldn't forget Gabriel's stark and heartfelt admission that her dancing that day had represented a freedom that he longed for—a freedom that 'no amount of money' had been able to buy for him. Had he been feeling trapped in some way?

She couldn't suppress the longing that infused her that one day he might reveal more of his innermost feelings to her—at least as a friend. It was easy to glean the fact that he was troubled. In the short time they'd spent together since his turning up at the door she'd begun to intuit that Sean's death wasn't the only grief that haunted him.

He didn't talk much during lunch, except to remark on how good the chicken salad she'd prepared was. Lara didn't mind. It was a glorious day and the warmth from the sun had helped ease any tension she might have felt because she was sitting opposite the man who had mesmerised her when she was just sixteen. The truth was he *still* mesmerised her. She'd fantasised about Gabriel so many times over the years—had even entertained the foolish hope that one day he might come back into her life, see the woman she'd become, and be enthralled by her.

But, seeing him again now, she knew that was just a pipedream. He was even more out of Lara's league than he had been all those years ago.

However, as they sat in the garden together she realised that the past association Gabriel had enjoyed with her and her family had definitely engendered an unspoken agreement between them that they could at least let their guards down enough around each other for a while and relax. They didn't need to present some awkward or uneasy façade that would prevent honest communication.

Reaching for the bottle of wine that she'd opened and stood in an ice bucket on the table, she poured some crisp white Chardonnay into their glasses and, raising hers in a toast, smiled. 'To old friends.'

A fleeting shadow passed across Gabriel's brilliant blue irises. His broad shoulders visibly tensed. Then he, too, raised his glass.

'To Sean, who once told me that the best bottle of wine was the one you shared with a trusted friend, whether it was vintage or a common or garden bottle of plonk.'

The expression on his sculpted, handsome face was indisputably wry, but it was tinged with a sadness and regret he couldn't hide.

'Your brother was far too generous. I wish I'd exhibited more of that quality towards him when I had the chance. But I was too set on carving my own path to properly consider him. I certainly wasn't around during the times he might have needed an ally or someone to confide in. Some "trusted friend" I turned out to be.'

'You're too hard on yourself, Gabriel.'

Not for a second could Lara deny the impulse that suddenly arose in her to touch him. God knew it was a big risk for her to give in to it, but she ached to give him some comfort. It was hard seeing him so down on himself like this.… Sean would have hated it, too.

Gently, she laid her hand over his. He stared down at it as though hypnotised. Then he shook his head.

'The fact is I'm not hard enough. I'm constantly creating strategies and contingency plans so that I don't have to face myself and confront the truth about who I've become…a man I'm hardly proud of.'

'But you've already told me what a success people think you are, Gabriel. You should be proud of what you've achieved.'

'So you think I've made a success of my life, do you?'

The pain Lara saw reflected in his gaze made her draw in a helplessly tight breath.

'What I think isn't as important as how you feel, Gabriel. You must have worked hard to get where you are, and you did it without help from either family or friends. That shows the kind of strength and determination that most people would love to have.'

'Does it?'

Shockingly, Gabriel seized her hand, as though he meant to make her his prisoner, and the intense, hungry glare he swept over her face made her heart thump hard.

'You're too damn generous for your own good, Lara. Let me put you straight about the kind of man I am, in case you're harbouring the belief that I'm somehow better. I'm *not*. I don't consider others. I'm a taker—not a giver, like you and your family. In the kind of world I inhabit the weak fall by the wayside and are quickly forgotten. I've had to learn to be tough. On the road to achieving what I want I've learned not to let anything or anyone stand in my way. If I come back into your life again I'm guaranteed to hurt you and make you rue the day you met me.'

Her mouth drying, Lara couldn't hold back the hot press of tears that surged into her eyes. His words had been like knives and her need to self-protect immediately kicked in.

'You're talking as if I'm nurturing some kind of hope that we might get together. Don't worry about that, Gabriel. I'm not.'

She sniffed and wrenched her arm free.

'New York has changed you, Gabriel—and not for the better. You used to be quite friendly and amusing. But it sounds like the path that you've chosen has corrupted you instead of made you happy. That worries me. And, just so that you know, I'm *not* looking for a man to be in my life. And I assure you that if I was I'm afraid it wouldn't be *you*.'

'Is that right?'

In a flash Gabriel was on his feet and yanking her up towards him, moving his hands down to her slim waist to hold her fast and pulling her against the iron wall of his chest. There was no time for Lara to think or even to feel alarmed. But her heartbeat went wild when his hand cupped the back of her head and forcefully directed her face up towards his.

Then the world as she knew it disappeared as though it was nothing but a hazy dream. Her eyelids shut tight as he crushed her lips beneath his, his hot silken tongue mercilessly invading and plundering the satin interior of her mouth in a kiss that seemed to be driven by passionate hunger and fury combined.

The frightening demand she sensed left Lara reeling. But it also stirred long-dormant feelings in her body, making them want to rise up and meet that furious hunger. Along with that shocking realisation there were other disturbing feelings and sensations that hit her. The foremost was how seductively delicious Gabriel tasted and how he exuded the most provocative scent—almost a primeval scent—that wasn't just down to the expensive cologne he wore. And the sheer strength of the man's hard, honed body against hers made her blood pound in her veins just as if he were some hungry lone wolf, intent on carrying her off to his lair to savour at his leisure.

But hers wasn't the only heart that was hammering. And when Gabriel suddenly and without warning let her go, cursing vehemently beneath his breath, Lara stumbled. Her legs felt as weak as strands of damp linguine.

Retrieving her balance as quickly as she could, she stood on her father's immaculately mown lawn and tentatively touched her fingertips to her lips. They were already slightly swollen and still throbbed from Gabriel's savagely hungry kiss. The man himself had already distanced himself and stood shaking his dark head in what looked to be disgust. When his gaze lifted to meet hers she had never seen an expression more nakedly stark.

'I'm sorry if I hurt you. Despite what I said, it was never my intention to do that,' he intoned huskily. 'But it's better you know now what I'm really like than find out later. At least now you have the chance to shut the door on me and vow never to see me again.'

Wiping the back of her hand over her tear-moistened eyes, Lara unflinchingly met his tortured gaze. It was then that she made a silent vow not to abandon him as his mother and uncle had done. Her friends might not have understood her decision if they'd been privy to his little speech about being 'a taker not a giver', but then none of them had known the Gabriel of old, and nor did they know how it felt to set your eyes on a man and believe that he might—*just might*—be your destiny.

Despite her private feelings about that, Lara was still determined not to let Gabriel have the upper hand. Even if she couldn't deny the powerful chemistry between them, she certainly wasn't about to let him use her and then discard her as if he wouldn't give her so much as a second thought. She didn't want to be one of the 'weak' that fell by the wayside.

'You probably didn't mean to hurt me, Gabriel, but the truth is you did. Perhaps you need to leave and reflect on that for a while?'

His glance was more than a little bemused. 'Do I take it that you'd be willing to see me again despite what just happened?'

'I would. But you won't behave like you have every right to kiss me like that again, Gabriel. Because I won't let you.'

Folding her arms across the fresh pink linen shirt that she'd donned after their walk as if she meant business, Lara sighed.

'I sense that you only did what you did out of sheer frustration at not knowing what to do with your feelings. Feelings that must have been building up inside you since you heard about your uncle and then about Sean. I can totally understand that. Grief can make even the most stable of people go a little crazy sometimes. It can make them act in ways they normally wouldn't.'

'So you think I kissed you purely because I didn't know what to do with my grief and went a little crazy?'

Sensing her face flooding with heat, she twined a long strand of rich brown hair round her fingers and unwaveringly met his gaze. 'Yes…yes, I do.'

'Then clearly you've learned nothing about men and their base desires, have you?' He raised a sardonic dark eyebrow.

Shocked more by his remark than by his rapacious kiss, Lara wanted the ground to open up and swallow her. Clearly Gabriel still thought of her as Sean's innocent little sister after all—a woman who had probably been sheltered from the world by kind but undoubtedly misguided parents and was consequently too naïve for words.

Gathering every ounce of determination and resolve she could muster, she refused to let his mockery get to her. Naïve or not, she still didn't believe Gabriel was displaying his true nature. Her intuition told her that presenting himself as cruel and uncaring was just a ruse. It wasn't the truth. She'd put money on it.

'I may not have a lot of experience with men, Gabriel, and I know it's been a long time since we last met, but I'm not as naïve as you seem to think I am. I'm quite aware of what goes on in the world, and of the— of the *desires* that people have. And, in spite of what you said, I don't believe that it's in your nature to take what you want just because you can. You've probably built a wall around your feelings for a long time, and it's only natural that those feelings should spill over since coming back home and being forced to face the losses in your life.'

She paused to take in a deep, steadying breath.

'I may not be as worldly-wise as you, but neither am I insensitive to the fact that you must be hurting.'

Even as she said the words Lara wondered how she'd dared express them when she saw Gabriel's lip curl disparagingly. He was rubbing his hand over the borrowed cobalt-coloured shirt that belonged to her father—a colour that brought out the intense glittering blue of his stunning eyes—and for a few heart-pounding moments she honestly thought he was about to walk away. To walk out of her life for ever.

'I hate to shatter another illusion, sweetheart, but I didn't kiss you because I was hurting.' Again Gabriel raised a rueful dark eyebrow. 'At least not in the way that you believe. I kissed you out of pure *lust*. If you find that shocking, then look in the mirror. The little girl that I once knew has grown up into a very beautiful and desirable woman. A very *sexy* woman. There's not a man in the world who would blame me for wanting you in my bed.'

'If you expect me to be flattered by that comment then I—'

He strode towards her again but Lara didn't flinch. Gabriel could taunt her all he liked, but she would stand her ground and refuse to believe him to be doing anything other than play-acting—seeking to divert her from the truth of what he was really feeling by making her think that he was a cold, heartless playboy with no remaining vestige of the friendly, teasing youth she'd known as a young girl.

'I don't expect you to be flattered, angel.'

Lifting his hand, he stroked his palm down over her cheek. The gesture both warmed and froze her at the same time. One thing she couldn't deny was the realisation that there had always been something unpredictable about his nature. Something *dangerous*, even.

Sean had once commented that women swarmed round Gabriel like bees round a honeypot because as well as having good looks he exuded a 'bad-boy' image they all seemed to find irresistible. Lara didn't doubt that was true, but she had never been frightened of him. She might be naïve, but she didn't think he would ever deliberately hurt her or cause her pain. Strangely, even his savage kiss hadn't changed her mind about that.

He sucked in a deep breath and the warmth of his ensuing sigh feathered over her cheek. It had the same startling effect as if she'd imbibed a shot of the most intoxicating brandy. The dizziness and weakness that flooded her made her wonder if her legs would ever hold her safely upright again.

'Rather than be flattered…for *both* our sakes…I'd prefer you to just tell me to go to hell and warn me never to darken your doorstep again.'

The exquisite carved male lips in front of her twisted, almost as if he wished she would put an end to his inner agony by readily acceding to his wish to tell him to go to hell. But Lara couldn't and *wouldn't* do it.

'No, Gabriel. I won't ever tell you that—not unless you deliberately cause me harm. Call me weak, or even stupid, but my brother would turn in his grave if I turned you away. My parents wouldn't be too pleased with me, either. I think our emotions have been heightened today because of what we've both been through….

losing people that we love. So let's put this upset aside for a while and finish our lunch, shall we? I've got some fresh fruit salad and cream for dessert.'

Feigning that she was unperturbed by what had just transpired between them, she lightly lifted Gabriel's hand off of her cheek and walked back to the table. But her heart was thudding like crazy as she pulled out her chair and turned back towards him. He was standing stock-still, staring at her as if he couldn't begin to fathom where she was coming from.

'No, Lara. I won't stay. Thanks for the lunch, but I think I'll pass on dessert.' He shrugged. 'In spite of what just happened I want you to know that I wish you a happy future—I really do. The *best*. I've no doubt you'll break a few male hearts along the way…that is, if you haven't done so already.'

Just as Gabriel finished speaking, Barney shot out through the patio doors like a bullet from a pistol. Fresh from the nap he'd been having after their woodland walk, he made a direct beeline for Gabriel, jumping up at him and yapping wildly with excitement as if he was his new best friend.

Lara could have kissed the terrier because, taken by surprise and with his defences down, Gabriel immediately dropped down to his haunches and appeared to gladly make a fuss of the animal. The action was just what was needed to defuse the tension between them.

'I think he likes you.' She smiled. 'I don't think he's going to easily let you go, Gabriel.'

'And how about *you*, Lara? Are you going to easily let me go?'

Even across the expanse of lawn that was between them the diamond glitter of his eyes seemed to burn a hole right through the centre of her soul, and it shook Lara. Licking lips that were suddenly achingly dry, she smoothed a tremulous hand down the front of her jeans and made herself hold his gaze unwaveringly.

'Probably not. I'm a bit like a terrier, too, when it comes to my friends. It takes a lot to shake me loose. By the time you go back to New York you'll probably be heartily sick of the sight of me.'

'You think?'

Lifting a joyful Barney into his arms, Gabriel rose to his full height again. The maddeningly enigmatic smile on his face made her limbs feel as insubstantial as cotton wool.

'Let's have that dessert now, shall we?' she suggested, aiming for a matter-of-fact tone and fearing she'd completely missed the mark. 'It seems a shame to let it go to waste.'

'Temptation personified—that's what you are, Lara Bradley,' Gabriel drawled huskily.

'I'd probably make a good saleswoman, then, wouldn't I?'

Hugging a now much calmer Barney to his impressively broad chest, he smiled. 'Sweetheart, you could sell me any damn thing you wanted and I wouldn't be able to resist. See how much power you have over me?'

If only he knew it wasn't *power* over him that she craved, Lara mused achingly, but something much deeper and more lasting.

CHAPTER FOUR

WHEN THE TIME HAD COME for him to bid Lara good-bye that day, his policy to keep them keen by not always being readily available—as was his habit with women—had made Gabriel strive to keep his tone and manner as non-committal and cool as possible. But all it had taken was one more lingering glance into Lara's big brown eyes to make him realise this was the *one* woman he wouldn't be able to employ his usual 'laissez-faire' technique with.

That incendiary kiss he had stolen from her might have left her thinking what a merciless bastard he was, but it hadn't been planned. He'd never known a hunger and a need for a woman like it, and in the midst of his surprising need to confess how driven he'd become in his bid for success his desire for her had reached fever pitch.

Add to that the fact that he had been mad at himself, mad at the world, and mad at the cards that fate had dealt him and it had been a recipe for fireworks. Now Gabriel couldn't get the taste of her or the memory of her soft and shapely contours out of his mind.

Realising he didn't want to leave before spending some proper time with Lara, he'd decided he would just let things unfold naturally between them instead of sabotaging his chances by being overly demanding and dictatorial. With that in mind, he had suggested that after his meeting with his uncle's solicitor the next day he pick her up and take her with him to see the house he'd been bequeathed, show her around. Somehow the thought of visiting his old home with her by his side was altogether more appealing than if he confronted the bittersweet memories it would undoubtedly evoke on his own. After the visit he would take her back to her parents' house so that she could walk Barney, and then in the evening he would take her out to dinner.

After hearing her gladly acquiesce to both those suggestions, Gabriel had left Lara to drive back to his hotel in Park Lane with his spirits raised even when by rights they shouldn't be—because not only had he lost Sean but he still had to face the ghosts of his past back at the manor house he'd grown up in.

That aside, he'd begun to sense that he and Lara had some 'unfinished business' between them. Why else would they have this chemistry after not even setting eyes on each other for years? Gabriel knew that he wouldn't be returning to New York any time soon without discovering the reasons for it.

'Do you mind if I ask you how your meeting with the solicitor went?'

In the sleek black luxury saloon car that Gabriel had hired for the duration of his stay Lara's tone was cautiously measured, as if she was unsure of what kind of response she would get from him. Gabriel couldn't blame her for being wary after what had happened yesterday. But right then, despite being secretly thrilled that she was sitting beside him, smelling as fragrant as a rose and looking breathtakingly lovely in her strapless pink summer dress, a more disturbing topic was dominating his thoughts.

That morning he had discovered that there was a surprising codicil to his uncle's will. How it would impact on his life should he go along with it had presented him with a dilemma he'd never anticipated. It seemed there was yet another complication for him to confront and deal with. Dear God! Was he *never* to be free of the demoralising legacy of his past?

Swallowing hard, he deftly steered the car off the main road and onto a thoroughfare that he knew led out into the countryside. It was an all too familiar route— one that he had travelled many times as a boy and rarely with any pleasure.

After travelling for a while in silence, Gabriel finally turned briefly towards Lara and answered her question.

'The meeting went as well as expected, I suppose, if not entirely to my satisfaction. Anyway, you'll see the house in a few minutes and we can go in and have a look round. I'd like to check a few things over and you can come with me. Then we'll have a cup of coffee. I'm expecting my uncle's housekeeper to meet us. She still maintains the place for me and sees to its upkeep.'

'It must be very reassuring for you to have somebody you know taking care of it.'

Seeing they were approaching the long fir-tree-lined drive that led up to the house, Gabriel grimaced.

'I don't exactly *know* her. Her name is Janet Mullan and I only met her when I came over for my uncle's funeral. She's nice enough, I suppose. A cheerful sort. God knows she would have to be to have put up with my taciturn uncle for so long. He wasn't the greatest conversationalist, that's for sure.'

Beside him, Lara emitted a soft-voiced sigh. 'You've never told me what his name was…your uncle, I mean.'

The question made his stomach clench. He'd always made a point of not calling his uncle by his name, because dignifying the man with a personal address might have suggested that he'd mattered to him—which he expressly *hadn't*.

'He was called Richard Devenish—or, to give him his full title, *Sir* Richard Devenish.' He wasn't able to prevent the acerbic inflection that crept into his tone. Being the man's only kin—apart from his errant mother, of course—Gabriel might have inherited the title but it meant little or nothing to him. He would probably never even use it. If he did, it would always be a bittersweet reminder of where he had come from.

His pretty companion shifted in her seat, and he sensed her big brown eyes staring at him in what was likely disbelief.

'You mean to say that you come from landed gentry, Gabriel? I didn't know that.'

'Why should you? I've never advertised it.'

'Did Sean know?'

'I must have mentioned it to him once, because every now and again when we got drunk he'd give me a mock bow just to rile me. Neither of us took it seriously, though.'

'You sound as though it embarrasses you. To have a title, I mean. I don't understand.'

'No.' Staring out through the windscreen at the gracious and mellow redbrick manor that had materialised at the end of the drive, Gabriel felt his insides lurch painfully. 'And I don't suppose you ever will…not un-less I tell you. Anyway, we're here.'

Parking the car on the gravel and turning off the ignition, he turned towards Lara to survey her. Once again a rush of pleasure and a need so acute pulsed through him. It was hard to think about doing anything else but making love to her. The sleek bared shoulders in the fetching summer dress she wore didn't exactly help divert the idea. The way the bodice hugged her curvaceous breasts made it hard to look anywhere else.

'By the way…' He smiled, consciously changing his previously gruff tone to a gentler one. 'Have I told you how pretty you look today? That dress is sensational on you.'

Lara's small pink tongue slipped out to moisten her lips and the colour in her cheeks went from a beguil-ing tinted rose to a deep cerise. The desire that was already gripping Gabriel with a vengeance veered to-wards the painful.

'No, you haven't,' she answered. Clearly perturbed by the compliment, she quickly moved her gaze to make an interested examination of the imposing building in front of them. 'What an amazing house. It makes my parents' place look doll-size in comparison.'

'Yes, but I know which one I prefer.'

Before she could comment Gabriel put his hand on the door handle and stepped out onto the gravel, then he stooped down to glance in at her. 'We should go in.'

Last night Lara had found it nigh on impossible to sleep. She'd lain awake long into the night, thinking about Ga-briel and the fact that he was returning the next day. The shirt that he'd worn during their walk through the woods was draped over a hanger that she'd hooked on the back of the slipper chair by her bed. She'd washed and ironed it, but it still smelled indelibly of its owner, and every now and then Lara had reached out her hand to pull the material to her and sniff it, to remind herself of how compelling and sexy Gabriel's scent was.

She had also touched her fingertips to her lips as she'd recalled the devastatingly passionate kiss that he'd stolen. And every time she had done so it had been as though she lay close to a furnace. There wasn't a single inch of flesh on her body that didn't feel scorched by the man. Just the memory of his heated passion had the ability to arouse her more than she'd ever been aroused before.

Although the beautifully tailored white shirt that belonged to Gabriel was no guarantee that he would keep his promise and return, Lara had chosen to believe it was. Even a man as rich as Gabriel surely wouldn't want to lose an expensive shirt…would he?

She needn't have worried. Gabriel had indeed returned, as he had said he would. And if yesterday when he'd shown up unannounced at her parents' door had felt like a dream, then the surreal sense had definitely intensified today. Lara knew her brother's friend came from wealthy stock, but she'd had no idea that the house he'd grown up in was as grand and palatial as *this*. Certainly Sean had never mentioned it. Had her brother sought to protect the other man's privacy by keeping the information a secret? Lara wouldn't be surprised if he had. Sean had always been fiercely loyal to his friends. Especially Gabriel.

Janet Mullan, the housekeeper, was a diminutive and pretty woman of around sixty, with a wing of silver hair amid surprisingly dominant chestnut curls, and she did indeed turn out to be just as cheerful as Gabriel had said she was. Her twinkling blue eyes lit with pleasure when she greeted them at the impressive Georgian double doors, and she seemed genuinely pleased to see the manor house's handsome new owner.

Straight away she demonstrated her thoughtful nature. If there was anything she could do to help Gabriel or his guest feel more at home, she told him eagerly, anything at all, then he shouldn't hesitate to ask. Would they like some iced tea or a cold drink before they looked around? The news this morning had forecast a 'scorcher' of a day.

Glancing briefly at Lara, Gabriel saw that she was happy to agree with his decision and declined. However, he did request some coffee and biscuits for after they'd finished touring the house.

After he had requested the key to his late uncle's study, because he needed to look at some correspondence that had been left for him, it was clear to Lara that her companion was restless, and she had the sense that Gabriel didn't want to spend any more time at the house than he absolutely had to.

It was hard to understand when he was now master of this incredible property.

When Janet Mullan returned with the key he politely thanked her and, touching his hand to Lara's back, partly exposed by the fitted pink dress she'd impulsively decided to wear that morning, Gabriel led her towards the palatial winding staircase that led to the upper floors.

After looking round several elegant and beautiful rooms they arrived at the light and perfectly propor-

tioned library. Lara had been wondering if Gabriel
would show her the bedroom he'd occupied as a child,
in the hope that it would give her a little more insight
into the man he had become, but she guessed he would
probably prefer to visit it on his own. However, as soon
as they entered the library, Lara fell silent in wonder.
She couldn't help it.

Before her were floor-to-ceiling shelves perfectly
arranged with books of every size and volume. More
avaricious and ambitious girls might dream of diamonds
and sports cars, but she would feel blessed beyond mea-
sure should she ever have a room totally dedicated to her
books, a room that she could read and relax in—even if
it was only small. Gabriel's library was beyond her wild-
est dreams, but she honestly felt privileged to see it and
to experience its gracious ambience, however briefly.

Catching what looked to be a rare pleased smile on
his handsome face as he noted her pleasure, Lara found
herself walking across the gleaming parquet floor to
the generous Georgian windows. Glancing out, she saw
that the beautifully furnished book-lined room looked
out onto a stunning river frontage, with acres of lush
meadow stretching further than the eye could see beyond it.

But she quickly set aside her pleasure at the view
when she realised that Gabriel had grown increasingly
quiet. Was he unhappy or upset about something? Lara
wished she knew specifically what was troubling him.
However, what she *did* know was that she could hardly
take her eyes off of him. Even dressed in jeans and a
navy blue T-shirt, with a casually open chambray shirt,
the man didn't look remotely out of place against the
impressive grandeur of his childhood home. Yes, Ga-

briel Devenish exuded class, whether he was conscious of it or not.

Yet the serious, almost solemn expression crossing his strongly delineated features didn't suggest he was remotely pleased at the fact that, as well as being a rich financier, he was now a seriously wealthy landowner, as well. In fact his preoccupied expression suggested he wished he were anywhere else in the world but here.

Just what was going through his mind? Was he remembering his uncle, perhaps? Yesterday he'd confessed that their relationship hadn't been a close one. For a boy whose mother had already abandoned him that must have been cruelly hard. Seeing his home again, was Gabriel perhaps regretting the now lost opportunity to make amends with his uncle and work towards repairing their estranged relationship? If only he would share some of his feelings with her.

'Gabriel?'

'What is it?'

Turning towards her, he pierced her with a troubled yet forceful stare, as though challenging her to say anything that displeased him. Lara didn't need to be a trained psychologist to sense that his composure was balanced on a precarious knife-edge. Now definitely wasn't the time to quiz him about his past.

'From what I've seen so far, this is probably my favourite room in the whole house,' she declared, endeavouring to convey an upbeat cheerful tone. 'How lucky were *you* to have had a personal library at your disposal growing up? If I had lived here I know this is where I would have spent most of my time.'

'Of course you would. That's why you became a librarian, isn't it? Because you love books?'

'I don't deny it.'

'Well, sweetheart…'

To her surprise Gabriel joined her at the window embrasure—but he was still looking troubled, and his compelling blue eyes had darkened like the precursor to a storm.

'Although you might think I was lucky to have a library and such a beautiful house at my disposal, it was anything *but* a pleasurable or happy experience. In fact most of the time the house felt more like a prison than a home to me. It wasn't until I went to university and met Sean, and then you and your parents, Lara, that I got a taste of how different my life could have been if I'd had a similarly happy family.'

Resisting the urge to touch him, even though she badly wanted to, Lara proffered a sympathetic smile instead. 'I'm sorry that you didn't experience a happy family life when you grew up—I really am. But I hope you know that my parents and Sean practically thought of you as family. Mum and Dad were equally as pleased for you when you graduated as they were for Sean.'

'And what about you, Lara?'

Gabriel startled her by reaching out to coil some burnished strands of her silken dark hair round his fingers.

'Did *you* regard me as practically family, too?'

Even though her heart slammed hard against her ribs, and her mouth dried uncomfortably, she bravely met his searing intense gaze without glancing away. It was clear that her answer was important to him and it behoved her to tell him the truth, come what may.

'No, Gabriel. I can honestly say that I never thought of you as family.'

There was a definite hitch of surprise at one corner

of his sublimely carved mouth but he maintained his steady, searching glance.

'Well, well...' His voice lowered meaningfully, and then he freed the strands of hair he'd captured and slid his warm hand beneath her jaw instead. Tipping up her chin to trap her gaze, he said, 'I have to commend you on your honesty, Lara. So, if not family then what *did* you think of me as?'

A sudden attack of nerves seized her. Running her hand down over her dress, Lara sensed it tremble. Gabriel's nearness and the seductive warmth that emanated from his body made it hard to think straight, never mind string a sentence together.

'I don't mean that I didn't regard you highly. Of course I did. You were my brother's best friend and I—and I thought a lot of you.'

'And how do you think of me now?'

She supposed the question was inevitable, but it didn't make it any easier to answer. 'I'm—I'm still fond of you.'

'Fond?' His fingers gripped her chin a little tighter. His blue eyes had never looked stormier. 'That's got to be the most insipid expression of feeling I've ever heard and I can't say that I like it.'

Lara shivered. Inside her strapless dress her nipples had tightened almost unbearably against her bra. They were like molten steel buds and they stung as though burned by a flame as she helplessly watched Gabriel's mouth descend towards hers.

An instinctive need for self-preservation, along with the need to maintain a modicum of equilibrium before she found herself irretrievably lost, swept over her and she found herself halting his lips' descent by laying her hand flat against his chest to stop him. It felt like an impenetrable iron wall, and even as Lara halted him her body clamoured feverishly for his touch.

'We shouldn't— We shouldn't be doing this, Gabriel,' she breathed.

'Says who?' One corner of his devilishly teasing mouth twisted wryly and he caught the hand that was attempting to stop him and lightly threw it away. Then he crushed her against him without the slightest remorse. 'If it's what we both want, then who's to say we should stop?'

Again Lara made a last-ditch attempt to utilise common sense. But Gabriel's desire had lit hers like a flame to touch paper and being sensible was the last—the *very* last—thing her inflamed body wanted to do.

His hard, honed physique felt incredible, pressed up close to hers, and it was clear he was aroused. But somehow she managed to tell him shakily, 'What I want is to be your friend, Gabriel...a *good* friend—not one of the "pretty ladies" with whom you spend the night when you want some company. Our friendship means a lot to me. I wouldn't want sex to cheapen it.'

He immediately dropped his hands down by his sides, looking stricken. Then he looked furious. 'So you would feel cheap if you slept with me, would you? I can't say that does a hell of a lot for my ego. But perhaps in the fairy-tale world that you inhabit, Lara, you were hoping for some kind of knight in shining armour to bed you?'

Gabriel swallowed hard, and his fierce expression was disparaging.

'Well, that's *never* going to be a role I can play, sweetheart, and if all you want is a friend then I suggest you look elsewhere. It's not as if you don't know my history and what a lousy friend I was to your brother. Why would you think I'd behave any differently towards you?'

It was inexplicable why she was so prone to make him angry, but rather than try to understand it right then Lara preferred to try and get to the root of why he was so furious. In spite of his rejection all those years ago, she honestly didn't think it was because he disliked her.

'My statement about sex cheapening our relationship came out all wrong, Gabriel....' She chewed her lip in frustration. 'I didn't mean that the act would make me *feel* cheap—it's just that it would be a shame to reduce the quality of the long-held regard we have for each other just because we succumb to a desire that might be quickly forgotten and...' Her face flamed red as she said the next words. 'And regretted.'

His answering frown was formidable. 'So you think I'd be such a lousy lover you'd immediately regret it?'

Lara could hardly believe how adept she was at saying the wrong thing sometimes. Briefly glancing out of the window and wishing for some kind of mystical inspiration, she couldn't help sighing. 'I don't think that at all. You—you seem determined to misunderstand me.'

Folding his arms across his chest, Gabriel gave her another long, examining look. The sun streaming in through the window behind him made his chestnut hair glisten like copper and she found herself transfixed by the sight.

'Then tell me this,' he said soberly. 'Do you believe there's something wrong with succumbing to desire? Do you think you'll be somehow punished for giving in to it?'

'I'm not some kind of nun who's taken holy orders, Gabriel.' Feeling uncomfortably foolish, Lara flushed.

'Excuse the pun, but thank God for that,' he commented drolly, making her immediately feel weak again when his mouth curved into one of his devastating smiles.

'Is there anywhere else in the house you'd like to show me?' she said quickly, moving across to the door and impulsively taking the opportunity to put some distance between them in a bid to try and calm her wildly beating heart.

With a wry shake of his head he replied, 'That could easily be misconstrued as a leading question, sweetheart, and to save your very charming pretty blushes I'll keep the answer for later. Right now I need to go to my uncle's study and look over some papers. Think you can make your way back downstairs, find Mrs Mullan and ask her to make that coffee for us? Hopefully I won't be too long.'

'Of course.' Feeling glad of the temporary reprieve, in order to get her thoughts together, Lara was happy to agree. But then a thought occurred. *What if the correspondence his uncle had left for him upset or distressed him?* What kind of mood would he be in when he returned downstairs? And would she be able to handle it adequately and give him the support that he might need?

CHAPTER FIVE

APPROACHING THE REGENCY-STYLE oak desk in a room that was imbued with the familiar scent of Havana cigars, Gabriel stared down at the cream vellum envelope with his name on it that sat atop the green baize blotter and unconsciously clenched his fists. Recognising the imposing inked script with the letter 'G' curled with an exaggerated flourish as his uncle's hand immediately made him shudder.

He'd been instructed by his uncle's solicitor that a letter would be waiting for him back at the house and had been asked to read and digest its contents as soon as possible in order to help make up his mind about the unexpected demand in the codicil.

Having already had that document meticulously outlined to him by the solicitor, Gabriel was in no mood to read what would in all likelihood be another disagreeable demand. He'd quickly learned that inheriting the manor was not going to be the straightforward formality that he wanted it to be. But at the end of the day he was an astute businessman as well as a banker, and it just wasn't in him to relinquish the desire to add to his already considerable fortune if the opportunity presented itself, no matter how testing the task would be.

Having seen the house and its extensive grounds again, he was already certain that he would put it on the market and sell it as quickly as he could before returning to New York. He certainly didn't want to take up residence here for six months in order to decide what he was going to do with the place, as the codicil stipulated he would have to if he wanted to inherit.

Had his uncle seriously thought that he would? He was sick and tired of being tied to the unhappy childhood memories that dogged his adult life. The sooner he was rid of the house the better. At any rate, Gabriel knew he could hire the best damn lawyer in the business to help him get round that particular complication. And he personally knew of at least two property developers who would all but rip off his arm to get their hands on the place as soon as they got wind that he was selling it.

He didn't feel an ounce of loyalty either to his uncle or to his forebears when it came to making a profit from the sale. After all, what had his esteemed so-called family done for him?

Feeling impatient, because he'd much rather be spending time with Lara, Gabriel tore open the envelope, unfolded the enclosed letter and hurriedly scanned it.

His heart was thumping hard in shocked disbelief before he even got to the end of the first paragraph.

Dear Gabriel
If you are reading this letter then it must be because I am no longer here. Knowing that must be the case, it behoves me to finally tell you the truth about your mother, Angela. She did not wilfully abandon you, as I once told you. That is the

first important thing for you to know. The second is the tragic fact that my beloved sister took her own life.

She had a serious depressive illness that there was no known cure for, and shortly after you were born it became apparent that she was unable to take care of you by herself. She herself needed round-the-clock care and supervision because her illness drove her sometimes to harm herself and her pregnancy exacerbated the tendency.

I lived in fear that she would harm you, too, Gabriel, although with hindsight I should have known that she adored you and would have protected you from harm with her life.

It was a wretched disease that she endured, and I told you that she abandoned you because she begged me to do so should anything happen to her. She was convinced it would be better if you believed that rather than knew that she was sick. She feared that you would get it into your mind that you might have inherited the affliction and that it would stop you from having the successful and happy future that she envisaged for you.

As for your father—I honestly don't know who he was, Gabriel, because Angela would never say. She did tell me once that she loved him, and that he was good to her, but also that he was married. When she knew that she was carrying you she broke off all contact with the man, and I stopped asking her about him because I could see that it distressed her.

I have not been as good an adoptive father to you as I should have been, Gabriel. I know that

*now and I deeply regret it. But my own father was
an austere and uncommunicative man who never
displayed much emotion and I suppose I must
have picked up the traits. Consequently I fooled
myself into thinking that if I provided every material asset you would need to help you get on in
life that would be enough. But the truth is because
of my own emotional inadequacy I denied you the
one thing that you perhaps needed the most—love
and friendship.*

*I will never know if you can find it in your
heart to forgive me for the tragic lie that I told
you about your mother, Gabriel, but I hope that
given time, if you do, then my beloved sister and
I will rest in peace.*

*Look after the manor house for us, my boy,
and fill it with your own dear children. One day
the sadness and pain that has hurt us all beyond
imagining will, I hope, be banished for good and
be replaced with sunshine and laughter instead
of heartache.*

*I did you another grave disservice, Gabriel. I
once told you that money would buy you anything
you wanted—even love. I was wrong. I hope you
know that now and can find the woman of your
dreams to make a life with. Home and family—
that's where true happiness lies.*

Sincerely

Your uncle, Richard Devenish

As he finished reading, Gabriel felt numb to his very
core. The sensation was quickly replaced by a sense of

rage and despair the magnitude of which he had never experienced before.

With his hands shaking he watched the neatly folded letter slip out of his loosened grip and drop back onto the green baize blotter. Leaning forward to rest his arms on the desk, he dropped his head into his hands and squeezed his eyes shut tight. So many feelings, thoughts and sensations rose up inside him at the same time that he felt he would drown beneath the crushing weight of them.

Opening his eyes, he murmured, 'Dear God—why hit me with this now, after all these years? It just doesn't make sense. It makes no sense whatsoever!'

Unable to stay still for a moment longer, Gabriel shot to his feet, heedlessly scraping the chair against the immaculate parquet floor. Vacating it, he furiously kicked at one of the legs and it crashed to the ground and lay on its back like a floundering whale. He had no inclination to set it right again.

It was hard to breathe suddenly, and the desire to escape both the house and the shocking truth of his tragic past was strong in him—too strong to be overcome or ignored. Snatching up his uncle's letter, he slammed out of the room and hurried downstairs.

'Gabriel, please don't drive so fast!' Genuinely frightened at the speed at which her companion was taking the narrow country roads, Lara felt her spine rigid with tension. But she was even more perturbed by the furious tight-lipped expression that hadn't left his face since he'd sought her out in the kitchen, where she'd been talking to the housekeeper, and unceremoniously declared that they were leaving right away.

'But what about your coffee and biscuits, Mr Devenish?' Janet Mullan had asked mournfully, clearly concerned that her new boss wouldn't be staying for refreshments after all.

Gabriel had looked even more irritated, and his tone had been surly. 'Don't stress about it. I'll be in touch again soon, to let you know what I'm doing. Just do your job and take care of the place in my absence. That's all you need be concerned about, Mrs Mullan.'

And with that he'd grabbed Lara's hand and urged her towards the door without pausing even once to explain why.

Lara had already guessed that he'd discovered something in his uncle's study that had disturbed him. He *must* have, she thought anxiously, because although he'd been a little quiet he'd seemed more or less okay before he'd gone in there.

'I'll get you home safely—you don't have to worry,' he said now.

His classic chiselled profile was as coolly perfect as one of Rodin's marble sculptures and he didn't even steal a momentary glance round at her.

Twisting her hands together in her lap, Lara sucked in a breath and answered, 'I'm not worrying so much about your driving, Gabriel, as about your state of mind.'

'What the hell do you mean by that?'

This time he did deign to glance at her, and his crystalline blue eyes were fierce.

'I mean I can see that you're upset, that's all. Why don't we stop somewhere and talk? It's not a good idea to drive when you're feeling distressed.'

'Why don't you let *me* be the judge of that? And do me a favour, Lara—please don't treat me like I'm one of your family's infamous waifs and strays that you can pet and nurse back to health. In case you hadn't noticed, I'm all grown up now and I can perfectly well take care of myself!'

Gabriel was indeed 'all grown up now', she thought privately, but that didn't mean he had the tools to try and heal whatever had distressed him on his own. He at least needed to talk things out with someone.

Turning her head to glance out of the window at the verdant country scenes that flashed by, she hoped that perhaps later, when he'd calmed down a bit, there might be a chance of reaching him and getting him to confide what had so disturbed him when he'd gone into his uncle's study. She could only pray that an opportunity would present itself.

Back at her parents' house, as soon as Lara opened the door Barney leapt up at her, barking an enthusiastic greeting, his short tail furiously wagging as if she'd been gone for *years* instead of a mere couple of hours. As was her habit, she dropped down to make a fuss of him, tickling him behind the ears, stroking his back and talking to him as though he understood every word she said—which she didn't doubt that he *did*.

'Hello, you little scamp. Have you missed me? I know you don't like being on your own for long, do you?'

The terrier emitted a short, sharp yap as if to agree.

Staring down at Lara's slim back and silkily smooth bared shoulders in that far too alluring summer dress she was wearing, Gabriel couldn't help fantasising about how easy it would be for him to unzip the garment and, using every seductive technique he had—and there were *many*—coax her into bed with him, rather than let her waste any more time and attention on the family's dog.

He realised he was becoming more and more reluctant to leave the brunette's side for even a minute. And after reading the hauntingly disturbing contents of his uncle's letter he was in no mood to be on his own. The only thing that could possibly help ease his soul-deep distress was Lara, preferably naked and lying beneath him.

As if suddenly remembering he was there, she rose to her feet, her lips curving in a tentative smile. 'What are your plans for the rest of the day? Are you in a hurry to leave? Only I was wondering if I could get you a cup of coffee, since we didn't have one back at the manor house.'

Her comment couldn't help but raise Gabriel's hopes. 'Are you angry with me because I didn't stay at the manor longer with you?'

Her expression softened. 'Of course I'm not angry. I was just concerned because I could see that you were upset.'

'Nearly everything to do with that damn house upsets me. But that's not your problem, Lara. I'll make it up to you when I take you out to dinner tonight. I'll book us a table at the Dorchester.'

'You have nothing to make up to me, Gabriel.'

'Yes, I do.'

'In any case, shall we have that coffee now?'

Rubbing his hand round the back of his neck, Gabriel grimaced. 'I need something a lot stronger than coffee. Have you got any brandy?'

Absently smoothing back the curtain of dark hair that framed her face, Lara frowned. 'But you're driv-

ing back to your hotel at some point, aren't you? I won't
give you alcohol if you're intending to drive, Gabriel.'

'You really *are* a little Miss Goody Two-shoes, aren't
you? I bet you never once sat on the naughty chair at
primary school, did you?' he jibed, hating himself for
sounding so disparaging when she was only displaying
her natural concern for him.

But his ill-mannered retort didn't seem to faze her.
As she lifted her chin he saw her glossy brown eyes
were defiant.

'Call me what you will,' she said, 'but I won't col-
lude with any plan that might potentially harm you or
get you into trouble, Gabriel—however much you insist
on having your way.'

Not releasing her perturbed gaze, he deliberately
stepped towards her. 'What if I want or need some
help?'

He'd knowingly pitched his voice low to engage her
intimately, and Lara's sharp inhalation of breath immediately drew Gabriel's avid glance to her cleavage. He
witnessed the provocative rise and fall of her luscious
breasts in the fitted bodice of that sexy pink dress and,
God help him, what was a healthy male supposed to do
in such testing circumstances?

'What kind of help?'

A corner of his lips quirked in a teasing smile. 'I'm
sure you must know the answer to that by now, Lara.'

'You have a worryingly one-track mind—you know
that? Do you *really* think us being intimate is going
to help resolve whatever upset you earlier? Something disturbed you when you went into your uncle's
study—don't you think it might be more help if we
discussed that?'

'No, I don't. I'm far more interested in what's going
to help me right now, sweetheart. Not in what happened
in the past. And, yes, I really *do* think it would help if
we were intimate. The last thing I want you to do is
worry about what happened earlier. That's *my* problem.
Can't you stop trying to be Lady Bountiful for a minute
and just be a woman for a change?'

Her pretty face was immediately stricken. It was obvious he'd touched a nerve, but although he regretted
that he might have hurt her it didn't stop him wanting
to seduce her. It might not ease any of the devastation
he'd felt on finally learning the truth about his mother,
and the lie about her abandoning him that his uncle
had colluded with, but fulfilling the intimate connection he craved with Lara would go a long way to help
satisfy the burning desire that had mercilessly seized
him since seeing her again.

It was a carnal hunger that made it almost impossible for him to think about anything else but being with
her in the most intimate way. Had the woman put some
kind of spell on him?

'That was uncalled for, Gabriel. I'm just as much a
woman as you are a man and you damn well know it.'

Hands planted firmly on her shapely hips, her dark
eyes glinting with fury, Lara had no compunction in
displaying her temper—and in truth right then those
fulsome breasts of hers, along with her rosily flushed
satin cheeks, ensured she was a sight for sore eyes.

Gabriel couldn't help concluding that Sean's 'little
sister' had turned into a woman who would stir lust-
ful longings in a stone, let alone a healthy red-blooded
male. It was an honest-to-God mystery why she was
still single.

'And if your criteria for judging femininity means that a woman is only feminine if she agrees to have sex with a man when he tells her that he's "in need" then you're seriously deluded.'

'Of course I don't think that!' Now it was his turn to feel aggrieved. 'You make it sound like I'm some stranger off of the street, instead of someone who's known and regarded you since you were young. Is it so hard for you to believe that I'm attracted to you, Lara?'

Gabriel was finding it increasingly hard to tamp down his growing frustration at her reticence to be closer. Perhaps he should open up to her a little bit more? Let her know that he had just as much feeling and sensitivity as she had, even though he rarely displayed it? Could he risk revealing such a thing to her?

The thought instantly made him want to retreat in order to protect himself. What if Lara laughed at his confession and concluded it to be a cynical ruse he was using in order to persuade her into bed? What if opening up more personally to her turned out to be a colossal mistake he'd come to regret? He had never yet given a woman that kind of power over him and he didn't want to start now. If he couldn't seduce her with his usual prowess and the skill that was innate to him, then he shouldn't even waste his time trying.

Reaching out to push the door shut behind him, and unknowingly tantalising him with her alluring sun-kissed scent that reminded him of a garden full of honeysuckle, Lara sighed heavily.

'I don't want to argue with you, Gabriel, but I *am* going to make us some coffee. Then I really think we should sit down and talk.'

Frustratingly having to own to losing this particular

little battle, but reluctant to walk away, Gabriel ruefully shook his head. 'Okay, have it your way—at least just for now. Perhaps some coffee will help clear my head. God knows right at this moment it feels like a herd of buffalo are stampeding through it.'

'That's probably the jet lag. Unless you have some kind of cold or fever brewing? Let me see.'

Reaching up, Lara laid her hand against his forehead, as if to ascertain his temperature, and her silkily cool touch made Gabriel suck in a surprised and pleased breath. It renewed his hope that she would continue to play nurse should he stick around a bit longer.

'You feel a little warm, but I don't think it's anything to worry about. If you start to feel any worse I'll give you something to help take your temperature down.'

'It won't work.'

'Why?'

'Let's go and have that coffee and maybe I'll tell you.'

Finding a perfectly legitimate excuse to touch her, when it was becoming more and more difficult for him *not* to, Gabriel slid his hand beneath her elbow to lead her down the hallway and out into the kitchen.

CHAPTER SIX

IT WAS ONE OF THE hardest things Lara had ever had to do—to sit down opposite Gabriel at the kitchen table and try to pretend she was impervious to the naked longing in his eyes. It would be so easy to give him what he wanted, what *she* wanted, too. But then what would that achieve other than fulfilling their mutual need for sexual gratification?

She didn't doubt he could get that anywhere. After all, what woman in her right mind could look at the man and *not* imagine what it would be like to make love with him? Never mind get the chance to actually find out! He was pure erotic female fantasy come to life. But although the thought of her body entwined with Gabriel's was a dream she'd often fantasised over—one that she'd longed to make a reality—she wasn't about to diminish her fantasy with just one or two stolen experiences in bed with him and then have him walk away. Not when she yearned for so much more.

'Can I ask you why you wore that particular dress today?'

'What?' Startled by the question, Lara stared back into Gabriel's darkly captivating blue gaze and frantically wondered what to tell him.

The outfit wasn't her usual style—that was for certain. When it came to more 'dressy' items of clothing she usually erred on the side of caution—not too revealing and not too showy. But her friend Nicky had persuaded her that this dress looked 'hot' and would be perfect for when she found herself going on a special date with someone.

She supposed that when she'd known she was seeing Gabriel the following day, and that he would be taking her to visit his ancestral family home, she'd decided it *could* constitute as a sort of date. Now, in the cold light of day, having his heated gaze examine her as if he'd like to peel off everything she was wearing, preferably slowly and stitch by stitch, Lara wished she'd been more sensible.

'I knew it was going to be a hot day, that's why.' She shrugged her shoulders as though it was scarcely worth even commenting on.

'Well,' he drawled, leaning across the table to pin her with a tantalising gaze it was impossible to wriggle out of meeting. 'I'd like to commend you on your choice. It shows off your figure to perfection.'

'Gabriel?'

'Yes, Lara?'

'I think we need to change the subject and talk about what's been troubling you. Can we do that?'

The answering scowl on that handsome hard-jawed face was not dissimilar to that of a small boy denied a treat. Under different circumstances Lara might have found it amusing. But she was becoming very familiar with Gabriel's avoidance tactics, and right at that moment she would have been hard-pushed to raise even the smallest of smiles. Not when anxiety about him was gnawing away at her.

'I know you probably think I'm being a bit too pushy, but I'm concerned. If you don't at least share with me what's troubling you then who *will* you share it with?'

Lifting his mug of coffee to his lips, he took a sip, then returned it to the table. 'So you want to hear the whole sorry tale of my hopeless and hapless family, do you?'

Straight away Lara registered the pain in his voice that he'd obviously hoped to conceal with self-deprecating mockery. Her heart twisted as apprehension and fear about what he might be going to reveal invaded her. She nodded slowly.

'All right, then.' Even though he'd agreed, Gabriel looked far from easy and stared down at the floor. 'My uncle left me a letter revealing things about my mother that I never knew.'

The words were followed by a near deafening silence that told her his feelings must be in utter turmoil. Somewhere outside a bird sang. The lyrical sound pierced the air, adding a heartrending poignancy to the moment.

Wanting to encourage him to resume his story, and fearing he wouldn't because the prospect of revealing his family secrets and potentially making himself vulnerable was something he no doubt despised, she remarked quietly, 'You said she left when you were very young. You don't remember her?'

He lifted his head. 'No, I don't. In any case, it turns out that that was a lie.'

'I don't understand.'

Gabriel's carved mouth twisted bitterly. 'Oh, she left, all right.'

He stared at her, lost in some unhappy reverie that he was still trying to make sense of, she guessed.

'She killed herself.'

Lara could scarcely think straight above the sonorous thump of her heart. 'Oh, Gabriel, I'm so sorry.'

As his confession sank in she felt even more stunned and sorry. She couldn't begin to imagine what it must be like to hear that your mother had committed suicide. How did a child—a child who was now an adult—pick up the pieces of his life and live anywhere *near* normally again after learning such devastating news?

Gabriel shook his head as though bemused. 'My uncle told me that she left because she didn't think she was cut out to be a mother. That was the story she begged him to tell me so that I wouldn't try and find out the truth about her.'

'But why—why would she do such a thing?'

Shrugging his big shoulders, the gesture momentarily straining the soft blue chambray of his shirt, he grimaced. 'He said it was because she was suffering from a depressive condition that was incurable. She was afraid that if I knew the truth I might think I'd inherited it and it would ruin my life.' A harsh semblance of a laugh left him. 'She must have really been disturbed if she thought it was better that I believed she'd deserted me!'

Leaning forward, Lara studied Gabriel as if seeing him for the very first time. There was no hiding his distress. She had a heartrending glimpse of the small boy who'd grown up believing that his mother hadn't wanted him and had consequently abandoned him. With every fibre of her being she longed to go to him and draw him into her arms. But she sensed there was a lot more yet to this terribly sad story.

'It sounds as though she was just trying to protect you, Gabriel,' she remarked softly.

'Protect me? From what, exactly? Her love and devotion?' His tone was bitterly disparaging. 'I may not be parent material, but I'm damn sure mothers are supposed to love and care for their children—not just abandon them on some whim!'

Several thoughts jostled for position in Lara's mind just then, but the strongest was her musing that if his mother had been mentally ill, then it was surely no 'whim' that had driven her to insist that her son didn't know the truth about her condition. The poor woman must have really believed it would hurt him.

But she didn't share the thought with Gabriel right then. The clenched fists he'd laid on the table and the tortured look in his eyes told her it was best to stay silent and simply allow him to express how he felt without interrupting the flow of pain and anger that must be coursing through him. Better that he let it out than keep it all in. Afterwards, bit by bit, Lara would do her utmost to try and help him.

'My uncle said in his letter that she'd been a danger to herself but he honestly believed she never would have harmed me. Did he think that would be a consolation when I learned that she'd killed herself? Did he never consider the effect it might have had on me, growing up believing that she'd left because she didn't want me?'

'Oh, Gabriel…'

It was no good. It was impossible for Lara to remain sitting in her chair when his feelings were clearly tearing him apart and she ached to console him. But when she got up and dropped her arm gently round his shoulders she sensed them instantly stiffen.

'Didn't I tell you not to treat me like some waif or stray that needs your help?' he growled, catching hold of her hand and gripping it.

Staring back into the starkly haunted blue eyes, she felt an answering quiver that was part fear and part desire run down her spine.

'I don't regard you as some kind of waif or stray, can't you see that? You're not a stranger to me, Gabriel. I'm treating you like I would any dear friend who needed my comfort and support.'

'So it's back to us just being friends again, is it?'

Her action purely instinctive, Lara retrieved her hand to lay her palm against his smoothly shaven cheek. His skin felt like sensually roughened velvet. 'Everyone can use a friend, can't they?' she breathed.

She didn't plan for her voice to catch on the final two words but it did. Even as she saw the pupils in Gabriel's blue eyes darken and flare she suddenly knew that it wasn't just comfort she wanted to dispense. Right then she needed him as much as he needed her and it was impossible to deny it.

'No, Gabriel, not just friends.'

In less than a heartbeat his big firm hands pulled her down onto his lap and without preamble he drove them deep into her hair. Although his warm breath fanned her face like a spine-tingling summer breeze, it still made Lara shiver.

'I want you so much I think I'll die if I can't have you,' he declared.

His voice was low and deep, the unfettered emotion it expressed so raw that it almost took her breath away.

Lara would have crumpled at the declaration if he hadn't been cupping her face and anchoring her. But his lips were against hers, his hot tongue invading her mouth and devouring her, and a low, hungry groan emanated from his throat that she couldn't help but echo as she surrendered to the irresistible fire that he'd ignited.

If it were possible she would kiss him for ever, she thought wildly, yet even for ever couldn't possibly be *enough*. Her hands weren't idle as Gabriel's lips worked their honeyed and stirring magic. They splayed out over the hard chest encased in sensuous cotton and chambray, her fingers helplessly curling against him in a voracious need to know and feel every part of him, to have the insatiable memory imbued in her mind and heart for ever.

Leaving her hair, Gabriel's hands slid down over her shoulders onto her back. Lara sensed his fingers fumble impatiently with her zip. As if shaken awake from a dream, she suddenly became aware that things were fast getting out of control.

Not wanting their first intimate exploration of each other to take place mindlessly and perhaps awkwardly on a chair, she twisted her mouth away from his and said, 'No, Gabriel, not here.'

Straight away she registered the confusion and protestation in his eyes.

Administering a reassuring smile, she gently extricated herself, then stood up and reached down for his hand. 'We'll go upstairs to my room,' she added softly.

'You're sure?' he murmured.

She hadn't expected to hear doubt in his voice, but doubt was what she heard—and it made her want him all the more because he wanted to make sure.

'Yes, I am. It's what I want, too,' she answered firmly.

Lara needed to show Gabriel that she was equally as aroused and needy as he was. She wasn't going to bed with him purely because she wanted to console him. The man turned her on like no other man ever *could*.

Rising to his feet, he impelled her into his arms as if he couldn't bear to let her go for even an instant. For Lara, too, it was difficult to contemplate leaving that safe haven when the familiar scent of his cologne and the arresting heat from his body made her feel as if she was, albeit briefly, abandoning a vitally integral part of her.

Staring down into her eyes as if he would see into her very soul, Gabriel loosely circled her waist with his arm. 'Then let's go.' He smiled.

The gesture was indisputably possessive and it thrilled Lara right down to her innermost core. Knowing that Gabriel really wanted her made her feel beautiful. How could it not when she'd loved her brother's charismatic friend from the moment she'd laid eyes on him all those years ago? There was an undeniable sense of inevitability about them meeting up again like this— as if they were meant to find each other again. Did Gabriel feel that way, too?

The seductive scent of her perfume lingered in the air as Lara took Gabriel by the hand and led him into her bedroom. The room was awash with afternoon sunlight but she made no move to draw the blinds. The most seductive shiver ran down Gabriel's spine as, instead, she led him across to a queen-size bed that was draped with a purple silk coverlet.

Truth to tell, it would have been difficult for him to note much else in that room other than Lara herself.

His blood was infused with a longing to hold her close so profound that it was as though he were caught in the grip of a dangerous fever that was steadily growing hotter. All he could think of to help ease his pain was getting her naked and joining his body with hers. And if he was seeking shelter from the storms of life that had battered him, seeking it in the only way he sensed might provide some brief respite, then he made no apology for it.

At the foot of the bed Lara turned to face him. Her silken dark hair framed her lovely face like a picture. Lifting her hands, she positioned them either side of his waist. As her melting brown eyes examined him it was as though she were touching him in the most intimate way. Gabriel burned to take her. But through the fog of his desire he vowed to take things slowly, so that the experience would be pleasurable for her. It would surely be worth the sacrifice.

Trailing his fingertips softly and deliberately over her mouth, he said, 'Will you undress or do you want me to do it for you?'

With a soft catch in her voice, she returned, 'You decide.'

He couldn't have wished for a better answer. Bending his head, he gently touched his lips to hers. As he did so he tugged at the zip at the back of the sexy pink dress and slid it down with ease. Momentarily breaking off the kiss, he stepped back so that he could tug down the bodice. The satiny material shimmered silkily down over Lara's bewitching form to the floor. As she stepped out of the dress she put her hand in Gabriel's to steady herself and then kicked off the cork sandals that she wore.

She lifted her head to study him. The undisguised need he saw reflected in her eyes all but undid him. He responded by deftly encircling her chest to undo the catch on her bra. When her beautiful breasts were freed, he was gratified that she didn't immediately try to cover herself.

For long seconds Gabriel just stared at her, drinking in the arresting sight before him as though not quite believing his good fortune. Then he put his mouth to one tip-tilted breast and suckled hard. Just as an electrifying bolt of heat ricocheted through his body and went straight to his groin, hardening him, Lara released a soft-voiced moan of pleasure.

Glancing up at her, Gabriel smiled. Flattening his hand, he laid it against her breastbone and gently pushed. As she gracefully fell back onto the purple counterpane the full extent of her curvaceous figure was at last revealed to him in all its irresistible glory. The luscious breasts with their peaked nipples, her slim concave belly and shapely hips, the silky smooth legs that were even longer than he'd imagined, the toenails that were painted with a sassy fire-engine-red.

After his initial heated examination Gabriel's thoughts were suspended as the urgent need to make love to her instinctively drove him instead. Tearing off his shirt and T-shirt, he jettisoned the clothing onto the floor. Ridding himself of his shoes and socks, he undid his belt buckle and left the belt to fall loosely against his jeans. Then he joined Lara on the bed.

He couldn't have said who welcomed whom first. The only thing he registered was their mutually ravenous need to hold each other close and be intimate. The rest of their clothes were quickly dispensed with as they embraced, and the vow he'd made to take things slowly fell mockingly by the wayside as soon as touched her. Ravishing her mouth more deeply and hungrily than he'd ravished any other woman's before, Gabriel ran his hands down over her shapely body and explored her. She was hot silk and sensuous satin, and the devastating revelation about his mother that had torn him apart that day freed some of its imprisoning hold on him.

When Lara disengaged her lips from his to whisper his name, Gabriel heard the unspoken invitation he was longing to hear and sucked in a shaky breath. Moving to sit astride her, his smile drowsy with pleasure and acknowledgment, he bent his head to continue the drugging kiss that he'd quickly become addicted to. Even as his mouth took hers captive he felt her silken thighs come round his waist to enfold him.

A second invitation was hardly necessary. He helplessly took her there and then, pressing himself deep inside her with a hungry primal groan. Her heat was like a honeyed river and Gabriel knew he would willingly drown in it—not just once but over and over until he was spent—until every hurt and bitter sorrow that had ever plagued him was laid to rest for good.

Lara had feared the relinquishing of her virginity to Gabriel. Not because she didn't want to lose it, but because she'd been afraid that the initial discomfort would prevent her from giving herself as wholeheartedly as she wanted to. But his heated sensual possession had quickly banished her fears. The most intimate core of her womanhood had softened so naturally to accommodate him that any discomfort she experienced quickly disappeared as she surrendered to the tidal wave of passion that consumed her.

But Lara did briefly wonder if, when Gabriel entered her, he had noticed that her muscles were a little tight— perhaps tighter than women with a lot more experience than her? She should perhaps tell him that this was her first time, but she was still wary of trusting him too much in case he either didn't understand or couldn't believe that she would wait so long to be with a man. If she were to confess that she only felt she could be intimate with someone she loved, would it scare him away?

The thought was swiftly quashed by the sensation of wondrous bliss and excitement that gripped her as Gabriel moved rhythmically inside her and her hands clutched the iron-hard biceps in his bulging arms to hold on. During that incredible, passionate ride Lara soon learned that imagination was no substitute for the breathtaking reality that was making love with a man she had been crazy about for years. Not for one second did he fail to live up to her hopes and dreams about the experience—in fact, he *exceeded* them.

As the heat between them gathered force Gabriel glanced down at her, his blue eyes blazing with hunger and desire as if there was no other woman on earth for him but her. It was then that Lara had to bite back her heartfelt need to tell him how much she loved him— how much she had *always* loved him.

She determinedly quelled the impulse as he moved deeper inside her and she wound her arms round his neck to pull his head down to hers. Even as they hungrily kissed, the need in her that had been helplessly building towards fulfilment suddenly reached its peak. She found herself on a trip to the stars that took her breath away, that made her feel mindless and boneless, that made her shake and quiver and cry out all at once.

Her heart thumped so loudly that she would swear Gabriel must hear it.

As she slowly came back to herself he gave her a lazy, satisfied smile, lowered his head and whispered in her ear. 'You're so beautiful you take my breath away.'

The edges of her lips curved in an answering smile and he lifted himself and drove into her even more deeply. Once again Lara had to hold on tight to the iron-muscled biceps as they contracted and grew hard beneath her fingertips. Then he stilled and convulsed with a harsh-sounding groan that seemed to emanate from deep inside his soul.

The sound made Lara shiver. It was as though every hurt and betrayal he'd ever endured had culminated in that groan and was now released. Feeling the hot press of tears against her lids, she wove her fingers gently through his hair and held his head, secretly thrilling that he stayed inside her instead of immediately moving away. Knowing he was a man who didn't trust easily, she was pleased and gratified that he must trust her enough to do that.

As he laid his head between her breasts, his warm breath skimming gently over her skin, she registered his racing heartbeat and murmured, 'It's all right, Gabriel, just let it all out. I'm here for you.'

He didn't look up, just stayed where he was, his body still as a statue. But Lara knew she didn't imagine the brief shudder that went through him or the near silent sob that was quickly suppressed in case she should hear it.

CHAPTER SEVEN

GABRIEL HAD NO IDEA how long he'd been sleeping. All he knew was that it was like the most delicious dream he could ever imagine finding himself waking up next to a softly slumbering and naked Lara.

Raising himself up onto his elbow, he gently moved the silken strands of dark hair that caressed the side of her face. She was lying on her belly, her lovely face turned to the side. At some point during the afternoon she must have pulled the purple counterpane over them, but it had slid back down to her waist to leave her back and shoulders exposed. It was then that Gabriel saw the perfect facsimile of an ebony and sky blue butterfly, whose delicate wings spread out over the base of her spine. The woman constantly surprised him. Who would have thought that the once shy young girl he'd known all those years ago would have opted for a tattoo, albeit one that only a lover would see?

Shaking his head, Gabriel breathed out a bemused sigh. But it was quickly followed by a stinging flash of jealousy. The thought of Lara being naked with another man, even if it *was* in the past, made him feel almost physically ill.

Making love with her had been one of the most ec-

static and meaningful experiences of his life since he
had shared some of the hurtful secrets about his past
with her. That had made the experience truly intimate.
Never before had he shared such personal information
with a woman. Shuddering, he remembered how he
hadn't been able to hold back his grief when he'd cli-
maxed—recalled too that Lara had gently advised him
to 'just let it all out' and told him that she was there
for him.

Then he remembered that he hadn't used protection.
It hadn't even crossed his mind. That was another first
and a not so acceptable one. Was Lara on the pill? Damn
it all, he should at least have thought to ask her. But he
had been so consumed by the fever of longing that she
aroused in him that rational thinking just hadn't been
on the agenda.

If she were to become pregnant after this, what
would he do? What would Lara *want* to do? Would
she agree to an abortion if he asked her? It was such
a shockingly disagreeable notion that a knifing pain
cramped his chest.

At that precise moment Lara stirred and opened her
eyes. Gabriel couldn't believe he'd forgotten for even
a moment how beautiful they were—dark-roast coffee
fanned by long, luxurious ebony lashes.

She was staring blankly up at him, as though caught
in a spell. Then her gaze fully registered his and she
asked softly, 'Are you all right? I mean, how are you
feeling?'

'I feel good,' Gabriel answered frankly. 'Better than
I've a right to, probably. I can't help feeling that I'm
very fortunate to have found you again, Lara. I guess
I must have done something right to please the gods.'

She dimpled. 'Maybe you're not all bad boy, then?'

'Is that how you see me? As a bad boy?'

'I think you have a little bit of that in you, but rather than detract from it, it just adds to your charisma.'

'Tell me more.' He grinned. 'I'm not averse to hearing about all the qualities that make me attractive to a woman.'

'What? And pander to your already inflated ego?'

Gabriel chuckled and realised how much he was enjoying just lazing in bed like this with Lara, in the middle of the afternoon, without feeling remotely guilty or having the need to get up and think about work.

'You don't have to do that to make me stay here with you, baby. Whatever you've got, I'm already addicted to it. That's why I'm still here.' Stroking his knuckles gently down her cheek, he smiled. 'You don't get rid of me that easily, either. I guess you're not the only one with a touch of the terrier in her.'

'Talking of which...' Lara sat bolt upright, grabbed the silk counterpane and pulled it up over her breasts. At the same time her cheeks flushed pink as though she was suddenly aware that she was naked. 'I've got to walk Barney. I can't believe I actually fell asleep in the middle of the day. I *never* do that—even if I'm exhausted.'

'This seems to be a day of firsts,' Gabriel observed smilingly.

'What do you mean?'

'It's not important.' Shrugging his shoulders, he levelled his gaze at her more seriously. 'However, what *is* important is the fact that I didn't use protection when we made love. That's a pretty major mistake, Lara, and whether you believe me or not it's one that I've never made before.'

Frowning, she told him, 'You don't have to worry, Gabriel. I'm on the pill. I should have mentioned it earlier, but we—I…' Her smile was a shade unsure. 'We got a bit carried away.'

Gabriel felt as if he'd been sucker-punched and didn't know why. Then he did. If Lara was taking the contraceptive pill then she must have the occasional lover. If she did, then it must have been quite a while since the last one, because she'd felt exquisitely tight when he'd entered her—as if having sex wasn't a regular occurrence for her. But the thought hardly reassured him. It made him feel disappointed, when in fact he should be grateful that at least one of them was taking the proper precautions.

Mentally gathering himself, he murmured, 'Thank God for that.'

Lara flushed and glanced away. Turning back to him, she asked, 'Do you know what the time is?'

He checked his watch. 'It's just gone four.'

'Four o'clock? You're joking?'

Amused, Gabriel drawled, 'Why the panic?'

'The panic is Barney must be desperate to answer the call of nature and I've got to go and have a shower.'

'That's an interesting dilemma. And there's one more thing you have to add to your list of things to do.'

'What's that?'

'You need to kiss me hello.'

Finally succumbing to the irresistible impulse that had been growing steadily stronger from the moment he'd opened his eyes and found Lara lying naked beside him, Gabriel put his hands onto her slim shoulders and pulled her against his chest. The silk cover slipped away from her breasts to expose them, and his senses were immediately aroused by the silken texture of her soft flesh and the peaked nipples pressing against him.

His blood thickened and slowed at the thought of seducing her again. Just as he was about to capture her lips in a drowsily sensual kiss that he hoped would be the precursor to so much more, right on cue the terrier downstairs made his presence known with a round of impatient barking.

'Oh, Lord. I'll have to go and see to him. I won't walk him—I'll just let him out the back. Sorry.'

With a sheepish glance, Lara wriggled out of his embrace and moved to the edge of the bed. Glancing down towards the floor, as though searching for something, she murmured an audible expletive beneath her breath and huffed out a sigh.

'What have you lost?' Gabriel enquired innocently, even as he reached behind her to pick up the bra and panties that had been partially hidden in the folds of the silk counterpane. He quickly slid them under her pillow.

'My underwear. But never mind.' Rising to her feet, she hurried across the room to grab a pair of jeans and a pink T-shirt from her wardrobe.

Transfixed by the wholly arresting sight of her bare bottom and long, slim legs, Gabriel found his gaze drawn to the exquisite butterfly tattooed at the base of her spine. Leaning back against the pillows, he drawled, 'I think this is the best wake-up call I've ever had. So what's the story behind the butterfly?'

Lara was in the midst of pulling up her jeans. She completed the task and turned round. The pink T-shirt she'd retrieved was held protectively over her breasts, as if it was still important to her to preserve her modesty even though she'd just presented an uncensored view of her delectable derrière to Gabriel.

'Sean sent me a picture of a butterfly just like it in his last letter home before he died. He told me it was extremely rare and that he felt privileged to have seen it.' With a nervous swallow she glanced briefly down at the floor. 'I suppose I had the tattoo done as a kind of homage to him. He often used to tease me that I "played safe" and didn't take enough risks in life. It makes me smile to imagine what he would have said if he'd seen it.'

'I think it's a work of art—and so are you, angel. You and the butterfly are an exquisite combination.'

'Thanks.'

The smile Lara gave him was so endearingly shy that it provoked Gabriel's carnal hunger even more. In fact he didn't know why he had even let her out of bed. Broodingly, he watched her hurriedly don the pink T-shirt she'd been holding against her. Braless, the garment was more revealing than she was probably aware. One thing was for sure: he wasn't about to complain about the fact.

'I'd better go and see to Barney. I won't be long.'

His mouth drying, Gabriel couldn't resist a final comment. 'So you're going commando, are you? What are you trying to do? Torment me? Do you know how close I am to hauling you back into bed?'

'If you do, then who's going to clean up the mess that Barney will undoubtedly leave on my parents' prized parquet floor? I can tell you now, Gabriel Devenish, it won't be me!'

In spite of his frustration Gabriel was still grinning at

the quick-fire remark, and devising lascivious ways he might repay her for it, long after Lara had left the room.

Gabriel's relief had been plain when she'd told him that she was on the pill and didn't have to worry. But as Lara stood at the back door that looked out onto the garden and watched Barney scamper across the lawn she knew he must assume she was a lot more experienced than she actually was.

What Gabriel didn't and couldn't know was that she took the contraceptive pill to help regulate her monthly periods and ease painful cramps. And, whilst Lara knew it wasn't a good idea to risk pregnancy when she wasn't even in a steady relationship, she couldn't help feeling regret that Gabriel probably would have hated it if he'd made her pregnant. After all, he didn't know how deep her feelings for him ran, or that she'd surrendered her virginity to him because he was the only man she'd ever loved and she loved him still. Trying to be realistic, she guessed that he probably wouldn't welcome anything that cramped his high-octane life-style—least of all a baby.

Determinedly brushing aside the moisture that surged into her eyes as she recalled how wonderful it had been to make love with him, she unconsciously held her hand over her heart. She still throbbed and tingled where he had touched her, where he had united his body with hers.

Although she'd naturally wanted to help give Gabriel the comfort that he'd needed after learning the devastating truth of how his mother had died, and how his uncle had lied to him to protect her, what Lara had said to him just prior to the event still held true. Their lovemaking had been something that she had wanted, too. Not just wanted but needed. Whatever happened now, or in the future, she would never regret it.

'*Oh, what a tangled web we weave when first we practise to deceive....*' The famous quote stole into her mind as she thought of the pain and distress the deception had visited on Gabriel—the pain and distress that would probably plague him for the rest of his life. Now he would quite likely sell the magnificent manor house he'd inherited because he would see it only as a lucrative investment he could cash in on and not as a family legacy he could be proud of. How could he when the wounds of his past were so great that no one would blame him for wanting to turn his back on the whole scenario? After he'd sold the place he would probably just return to New York and Lara would never see him again.

'No.'

It jolted her to realise she'd voiced the protest out loud. But already she was making a vow not to let such a bleak scenario occur if she could prevent it. Somehow there must be a way to get Gabriel to see the gift he would be turning his back on—the gift that might be the key to helping him heal the grievous wounds from his past and make him see that he didn't need to bear them for ever, that his future could be so much brighter if he would only give himself the chance to explore the possibility and not run away.

Lost in her heartfelt reverie, Lara sighed. Then Barney started to bark and she glanced down to see the terrier scampering past her, no doubt in search of his basket and a nap. It was then she remembered that Gabriel was waiting for her upstairs. She almost wanted to pinch herself to make sure she wasn't dreaming. It wasn't necessary. The stinging tips of her tender breasts where Gabriel had kissed and suckled them were an apt reminder that this was no dream but instead a heart-poundingly wonderful reality.

Hugging herself, she headed out into the hall and quickly returned upstairs.

To her surprise, Gabriel wasn't in bed where she'd left him. Just as Lara sensed her stomach plunge at the thought that he'd slipped away whilst she'd been keeping an eye on the dog, the en-suite bathroom door opened and he stepped out, fully dressed and combing his fingers through his lightly tousled chestnut hair. His charismatic smile was both rueful and rakish at the same time.

Before she could ask what was going on he strode over to her and possessively wound his arms round her waist. Even though his embrace instantly rendered her weak with pleasure and desire, Lara suspected her secret hopes about how they might spend the rest of the afternoon weren't going to come to fruition.

'What's wrong? Why—why are you dressed?'

'I had a phone call from New York while you were downstairs. Sweetheart, I'm afraid I've got to go back.'

'You mean back to New York?'

Grimacing, Gabriel nodded. 'They've got a real crisis on their hands on the trading floor. They want me to go back and help sort it out.'

'But what about the legalities you said you needed to deal with here? I mean the ones concerning the house?'

'They're just going to have to wait. Right now my priority is getting back to New York. The sooner I leave, the sooner I'll be back.'

Lara stared into his captivating blue eyes and couldn't help offering up a silent relieved prayer that he intended to return. But she still didn't want him to go. 'So you *are* intending on coming back, then?'

Lowering his head, he captured her lips in a slow, seductive kiss that melted her and made her long for more. The touch of his mouth against hers was oh so drugging and sensual that she thought there couldn't be a woman alive who wouldn't surrender to the magic of it without the heartfelt hope that there would be more—much more—to follow.

'Of course I'm coming back. Do you honestly think I'd turn my back on the treasure that I've found?'

'You mean your family's manor?'

Gabriel tipped up her chin with his knuckle. 'No. That's not the treasure I mean at all, angel.'

As Lara stared back at him her heart skipped a beat.

'You make it very hard for me to leave when you look at me with those big brown eyes of yours like that, but nonetheless—' He abruptly dropped his hand and said briskly, 'I'd better be off. I've got to get back to my hotel and pack a bag. Can you give me your phone number?'

Retrieving his mobile from his jeans pocket, he looked at her expectantly.

'What do you want it for?'

'Do you really need to ask me that? So that I can let you know when I'm coming back, of course.'

'Oh.'

The number duly given, Lara gasped when once again Gabriel drew her into his arms.

'I know you've only been back a short time but it's going to feel strange not having you around,' she admitted.

'I feel the same, sweetheart.' Smiling ruefully, he cupped his hand to her cheek. 'Now I really do have to go.'

He moved across the room to the door and opened it. Then he pivoted, and the expression on his carved face was indisputably serious as he glanced back at her.

'I don't want you to be lonely but I hope you won't think of being with anyone else while I'm gone?'

Feeling her cheeks flame red, Lara couldn't help but be offended. Her telling him she was on the pill had made him naturally assume she was sexually active. The thought made her shiver with distaste, especially when she had always believed that the most precious thing you could give to the man you loved was your virginity. Yes, the idea was outdated and old-fashioned but Lara made no apology for it.

'Do you honestly think I would want to be with someone else after what we've just shared, Gabriel? I know we haven't committed to making our relationship serious or anything, but I'm not the kind of woman who operates like that. I'm loyal. How would you feel if I asked *you* the same question?'

His expression thoughtful, he answered soberly. 'You need have no worries on that score. Apart from the fact that I'll be too busy working, the only woman I'll be thinking about while I'm in New York is *you*, Lara.'

She released a soft breath of relief and followed it with a smile. 'That's all right, then. Have a safe journey and let me know that you've arrived safely, even if it's just a text.'

The corners of Gabriel's eyes crinkled with pleasure. 'Of course. It'll be nice to know that someone I care about is thinking of me while I'm away. That's another first.'

Feeling elated by his assertion that she was some-one he cared about, Lara felt the rest of his poignant comment squeeze her heart. How had he felt when he was little and knew there was no one there to look out for him and give him a cuddle when he got home from school? A hired nanny could never have replaced a lov-ing parent.

Right then he looked so endearing that Lara won-dered how she didn't run to him and beg him not to go. But she knew that she shouldn't reveal that she cared as much as she did in case it made him want to back off a little. That was the very *last* thing she wanted to happen.

'Well, here might be another first for you, Gabriel. I'm really going to miss you when you're gone.'

He gifted her with another devastating smile that she wouldn't easily forget.

'I'm going to miss you, too, baby.' Raising a rueful dark eyebrow he opened the door and went out.

The days following Gabriel's departure dragged by in-terminably. Lara's initial excited optimism and belief that he would return, and that when he did he might consider making their rekindled association more se-rious, started to evaporate distressingly.

Since he'd texted her that he'd arrived safely in New York her mobile had been worryingly silent. To add to her worry and concern, memories of that long-ago party from her youth, when Gabriel had rejected her in pref-erence for the tall slim blonde who had been his tutor, returned to haunt her painfully and made her fear that he wouldn't keep his promise if someone more attrac-tive came on the scene when he was back in New York.

When her parents returned from France Lara stayed

on for a further couple of days to satisfy herself that they were coping and to give them whatever support she could. But she also stayed on because her family home now seemed indelibly imbued with Gabriel's presence. She almost feared to leave it in case it signified shutting the door on the magical and heartfelt time they had spent together there—a repeat of which might never happen.

CHAPTER EIGHT

IT HAD NOT BEEN the best of days. How could it have been when they were still experiencing the aftermath of a serious crisis on the trading floor and heads were starting to roll as some key players were called into account?

Gabriel had nothing to fear on that score—his record was exemplary and so were his dealings—but he still felt a huge responsibility towards the shareholders he had guided and advised. Especially when some of the companies he'd recommended for investment had gone to the wall during the past few days due, amongst other things, to bad management. God knew he'd warned the CEOs of said companies enough times that good management was key and they shouldn't be in a hurry to let go those with a proven track record in order to replace them with the current 'flavour of the month'.

But most of all it was a bad day because he couldn't be with Lara. He'd been back in New York for over a week now and already the separation felt interminable. As he had expected, work had consumed him.

Back in his high-rise apartment later that evening, he threw himself down on his opulent silk-sheeted bed fully clothed and mused on whether he should ring her just to hear her voice and assure himself that he hadn't dreamt the blisteringly hot connection that they'd shared.

The situation had undoubtedly rocked his world. When he'd read about Sean's death, Gabriel never would have believed that going back to see his friend's parents to offer his condolences would result in him meeting Lara again and finding himself insanely attracted to her. She had been a pretty teenager, but nothing could have prepared him for the stunning woman she'd become.

He'd since asked himself if he should actually be feeling guilty because he'd taken a long-ago friendship to a whole other level just because the opportunity had presented itself. But he hadn't been able to resist. After reading the gut-wrenching letter his uncle had left him which had revealed the tragic truth about his mother, Gabriel had found himself craving the kind of comfort that only a woman could supply. A lovely woman like Lara, whose caring and selfless nature was like a price-less gem that was rare to find.

Checking his watch, he noted that it must be about four in the morning over in the UK. Would he risk waking her from sleep simply just to hear her voice? Of course he would. Hadn't she told him when he was leaving that she would miss him? Well, now was a good opportunity to find out how much.

Sitting up, he undid his tie, then shrugged off the suit jacket he wore and carelessly threw it onto a nearby chair. Then he kicked off his shoes, plumped up the satin pillows behind him and rang her mobile.

Even the realisation that she would be asleep couldn't stop him from feeling impatient when she didn't pick up straight away. Holding the phone close against his ear, with his other hand he dragged his fingers wearily

through his hair, thinking that if he had even half a
mind to be sensible he should probably get some sleep
himself. He'd been working flat out in a charged and
nervous atmosphere since the early hours of the morning and felt like death.

But he instantly jettisoned the thought when he heard
Lara's sleepily husky voice at the other end of the line.

'Hello? Who is this? Have you any idea what time
it is?'

Gabriel couldn't resist chuckling. 'Who else would
be ringing you at this ungodly hour if it wasn't me,
baby?'

'Gabriel?'

He told himself he heard pleasure in her voice, as
well as surprise, but he couldn't know that for sure.
What if Lara hadn't missed him even half as much as
he had missed her? What if, despite her asking him if
he really thought she would want to be with someone
else after being with him, she had sought out the company of an ex-boyfriend to help alleviate her loneliness?

Biting back a savage curse at the mere thought, he
schooled himself to breathe more slowly. A potential
coronary wasn't something he wanted to add to his already considerable cache of woes.

'Yes, it's me.' Despite his anxieties, Gabriel thought
of her shining dark eyes and pretty face and his lips
shaped a smile. 'I should say I'm sorry for ringing you
so early in the morning, but if I were to tell you that
then it would be a lie. Were you asleep?'

'Not really. I was only dozing. I don't fall asleep very
easily these days. I just can't seem to settle.'

'Are you still at your parents' house?'

'No, I'm not. I've returned to my flat. Mum and Dad

came back from holiday a couple of days after you left. By the way, they asked me to tell you that they'd like to see you sometime. They've got a couple of photos of you and Sean they'd like you to have as a keepsake.'

Gabriel's insides churned at the prospect of meeting Lara's parents again when he had so recently seduced their daughter. Would he be able to handle the guilt that was bound to surface when he was in their presence? Their good regard had once upon a time been very important to him. It still was.

'It would be good to see them again,' he said warily. 'And I wouldn't mind having the photos.'

'Good. I'll tell them. Anyway, it's good to hear your voice. The last time I had word from you was when you texted me to say that you'd arrived in New York. How are you?'

'Never mind how *I* am. What do you mean, you can't seem to settle? Is there something on your mind? Tell me, Lara, I'd like to know.'

Registering her quietly indrawn breath, not for the first time Gabriel wished he hadn't left her so abruptly when he'd got the call from his office in New York. But when he'd learned his presence was urgently required because of a crisis that could potentially escalate if he didn't return and help resolve it, it had been unthinkable that he would refuse—especially when his professional reputation had been built on finding solutions that would fox many of his peers.

'I've—I've just been missing Sean, that's all. It's at times like these—times when I'm a bit low and down in the dumps—that I'd ring and talk to him. No matter what the situation he'd always help put things into perspective and make me laugh.'

'It's perfectly understandable that you're missing him, sweetheart. His death isn't something you're going to get over or come to terms with overnight. All you can do is to give it time. Isn't that what they say?'

'Yes, and isn't it ironic how plausible and sensible that sounds when it isn't someone that's personally close to you who dies?'

Dry-mouthed, Gabriel honestly didn't know how to answer her. He'd lost the one person who was universally meant to be the closest to a child, yet he hadn't known his mother at all. Not even for a little while. How were you supposed to grieve for a relative stranger? Because that was what she had been. Yet since he had found out that she'd taken her own life a sense of bitter sorrow at the futility of it all had slowly and undeniably crept into his heart and taken up residence there. Not usually given to fantasising, he had found himself wishing for the power to turn back time so that he might remake the past and ensure a different and better future for both of them. Perhaps he was experiencing grief after all?

He heaved a sigh.

'Gabriel? I wasn't being dismissive of your advice. I know you're dealing with your own grief.'

'Is that what you call it?' Even though he'd briefly flirted with the fantasy of remaking the past, he couldn't prevent the scathing inflection in his tone. 'What the hell would I know about it? Aren't you supposed to have a relationship with someone before you can grieve for them?'

'Just because you didn't have a relationship with your mother doesn't mean that you don't wish that you had. Look, let's talk about something else, shall we? Late at night, or even in the early hours of the morning, isn't the best time to be dwelling on things that make us sad.'

For a moment, Lara's gentle voice somehow subdued the influx of pain that had threatened to submerge Gabriel.

'And I hate to think of you being sad when you're so far away and I can't be with you to help make you feel better.'

'I'm not sad, for goodness' sake. I'm *angry*. Furious that the people who were meant to take care of me were such liars that they would deceive their own flesh and blood and not even consider the horrendous legacy that would leave me with. You can't possibly know how that feels.'

Shaking his head, Gabriel fought hard to recover his equilibrium beneath another crushing wave of emotion. What the hell did he think he was doing? He'd been longing to make contact with Lara for days—the mere thought of talking to her had been the light at the end of the tunnel when he'd been so consumed by work that there wasn't even a spare moment to ring her—and here he was, wasting precious time talking about his hopeless family.

He swallowed hard.

'Forget I said that, will you? I think it's just fatigue talking. Up until now it's been a hell of a day. But I already feel better knowing that you're thinking about me.'

'I'm glad. I know it doesn't solve anything, but it helps to know that you have a friend you can reach out to, doesn't it? I know it does for me.'

Trying hard to ignore the fact that she'd referred to him yet again as a friend and not as her lover—

had his lovemaking been *that* forgettable?—Gabriel sighed again.

'Look, don't you have some holiday left? Why don't you come over to New York for a few days?' Even as the idea made his heart race and his blood pump hard he knew it was a brainwave he couldn't ignore. Why hadn't he thought about it earlier? It was, after all, the perfect solution. If he had to spend many more nights without seeing Lara and having her in his bed he'd honestly go crazy.

'I do have some holiday left, but don't you have to work, Gabriel? Isn't there some big financial crisis or other you have to deal with?'

'There is indeed.'

The charmingly innocent question made him smile. The world Lara inhabited was a million miles away from the feverish atmosphere on Wall Street, where dealings often had serious global financial implications that could make or break economies overnight. He was fiercely glad that she wasn't part of that world.

He was also relieved that she wasn't remotely like some of the clever but brittle women he regularly came into contact with in that arena—women who had seemingly forgotten what it meant to be soft and feminine, who preferred to concentrate their energies on rising to the top of the career ladder, making their fortune, and didn't care what they had to do in order to achieve it. Some men might find such barefaced single-mindedness admirable, but oddly enough Gabriel *didn't*.

'It won't be sorted overnight,' he explained. 'But we're making some good inroads. Anyway, let's not talk about that. I really need to see you, Lara. You have no idea *how* much.'

The other end of the line went ominously quiet and Gabriel tensed. Her rejection wasn't something he wanted to contemplate even briefly.

'Say the word and I'll arrange the flight,' he said quickly. 'I'm not saying I'll be able to spend as much time with you as I'd like when you get here—especially not during the day when I'm working—but you'll have my driver at your disposal to take you wherever you want to go, and you won't want for anything. If you want to buy clothes, perfume—*anything*, in fact—I'll foot the bill. It will be my pleasure. And as often as I can manage it we'll have the evenings together. The nights, too.'

Again, Gabriel's blood heated at the thought. He blessed the photographic recall that, even throughout his pressured working days, helped him easily access the memory of Lara's seductive scent and the satin texture of her flawless skin.

'Are you sure, Gabriel? I mean, my coming to see you won't interfere with your routine?'

'My God, do you know how painfully dull that makes me sound? I don't deny that my work is important, but even *I* refuse to make it the be-all and end-all. Especially not now, when I know that I'll be seeing you.'

'All right, then. You can go ahead and arrange a flight for me. When you have the details you can ring or send me a text to let me know. My mum said just yesterday that I ought to have a holiday before I go back to work.'

'She was right—and if my memory serves me correctly your mum usually *is*, sweetheart.'

Rubbing his hand round his stubbled jaw, Gabriel was elated that his powers of persuasion hadn't failed him. If all went to plan Lara would be joining him in just a couple of days' time and his photographic memory would no longer be necessary to remind him of her charms—not when the delicious reality of her presence would be so much more satisfying.

Even though she'd accepted it—because what else could she have done?—Lara had been heartbroken when Gabriel had abruptly left her to return to New York. At that point she really hadn't known whether she would ever see him again. All she'd seemed to see in that carved, handsome face of his when he had announced he had to return to work to help alleviate a crisis was a man who put his career way above personal relationships and matters of the heart. *No question.* What if he had even felt *relieved* when he'd had the call telling him he was needed urgently?

Yet even knowing that Gabriel was a supremely driven individual, whose priorities were vastly different from her own, Lara didn't give up hope that one day soon he would come to see that there were far more important things in life than money and the admiration of his peers.

The devastation of his mother taking her own life and his uncle betraying him might have caused him to believe that love and family could never be for him—not when his trust had been so cruelly tested—but Lara refused to relinquish the hope that if only she could reach him—*really* reach him—then she might help him see that it didn't mean that love and family should be denied him.

It had lifted her beyond belief when he'd rung her in the middle of the night and invited her over to New York and she hadn't hesitated to accept the invitation.

Could it be that he'd been reflecting on the possibility of enjoying a serious relationship with her? She prayed that was the case. She certainly wasn't going to pass up the chance of finding out.

When he'd asked her what had been unsettling her she hadn't been completely truthful. Of course she was still grieving for Sean, but she'd also been missing Gabriel—missing him so much, in fact, that she could scarcely think about anything else.

Sometimes the memory of their lovemaking seemed like the most delicious dream she had conjured up to help compensate for the loneliness she had endured all these years. And other times, because it meant so much to her, it fuelled her fears about what she would do if she never got the chance to be intimate with him again. Lara had already lost the brother she'd adored. To lose Gabriel would be an equally grievous blow.

Now, travelling in the back of the beautiful limousine Gabriel had sent to the airport to collect her and heading over to Fifth Avenue, where his apartment was situated, Lara stared up at the high-rise buildings piercing the faultless blue sky and couldn't help shivering. It was as though she'd been dropped into an alien habitat in some distant universe, such was the contrast to the much more unhurried environment she was used to.

'This is it, Miss Bradley. If you tell the concierge at the door that you've come to see Mr Devenish, then he'll take you up to his apartment.'

'Thank you.'

'It's my pleasure, Miss Bradley. If you just wait there for a moment I'll get your luggage.'

When he came round to open the car door for her, Lara accepted the immaculately presented chauffeur's hand and stepped out onto the sidewalk outside the building. Already the concierge was approaching, and as she thanked the driver again she was rewarded with a genuinely warm smile.

'I'm Barry, by the way, and Mr Devenish will give you the number to contact me on when you want to go anywhere. He's already given me instructions to take you wherever you want to go during your stay,' he told her. 'So I'll look forward to seeing you again sometime soon, Miss Bradley. Have a good day, now.'

'You, too.'

It hit Lara then just how diametrically opposite Gabriel's lifestyle was to her own. She had just about got over travelling business class on the plane out here, but was he *really* expecting her to tour the city in a limousine every time she went out?

As the ultra-polite concierge took charge of her conservatively small suitcase and led her to the elevator she was suddenly seized by an acute attack of nerves. What would it be like, seeing Gabriel again? Would he still want her as much as he'd wanted her back home? Compared to the beautiful and fashionable women he must see every day at work, would he start to see her as painfully ordinary and homely? She glanced down at the royal blue, fluted-sleeved tunic dress she was wearing that she'd thought so pretty in the store and winced.

'This is Mr Devenish's floor, Miss Bradley.'

The ascent up to the top floor had been so swift that she'd hardly realised they'd been moving. She'd been too lost in anguished reverie about Gabriel.

The concierge pressed the doorbell and with a brief, officious smile asked, 'Would you like me to wait with you until Mr Devenish comes to the door?'

'No, thank you. I'm sure he'll be here in a minute.'

With a brief nod of his head, he left her. They had arranged that Gabriel would take a couple of hours off from work to welcome her and acquaint her with her new surroundings, but time seemed to deaden and slow as Lara waited outside the door for him, and she couldn't help worrying that because he was so busy at work he'd forgotten about her.

But suddenly he was standing there, immaculately dressed as ever, and even more devastating than she remembered. His eyes locked on to hers immediately. They drank her in, ate her up and all but consumed her, body and soul.

Lara opened her mouth to speak but no words came out.

Looking slightly dazed, he said, 'My phone rang just before you knocked and I stupidly took the call. My God, I've been waiting so long for you. Too long.'

And then further dialogue was abandoned as he hungrily drew her into his arms, drove his hands through her hair and pressed her against him as if she was as vital to him as taking his next breath.

If that first kiss he had stolen from her back in England had been akin to being scorched by flame, this one was an inferno that burnt her down to her very core. In response, her lips couldn't help but cling ravenously to his, and her heart leapt with sheer delight at the seductive velvety texture of his lips and the sensation of his hard body enfolding her. Then she greedily welcomed his hot searching tongue, taking breathless little gasps of air as she struggled to assimilate the tide of longing and desire that rendered her almost too weak to stand.

Gabriel groaned as if he couldn't bear being bereft of

her kisses for even a moment. Defenceless and desperate for his deepening touch, Lara was scarcely aware that he had dragged in her case and pushed the door shut behind her, then manoeuvred her up against it. But when his hand hotly covered her breast through the thin cotton of her dress, and when he replaced it with his lips to nip at the already tender flesh of her aroused nipple, she whimpered as an arrow of molten heat shot directly into her womb.

Even as she moaned her pleasure Gabriel moved his hands urgently down her back and onto her behind. In answer, Lara eagerly drove her fingers through his hair to hold him more tightly against her. A second later, he freed himself to examine her. As she met the intense azure gaze that had instigated her love and devotion all those years ago when she was not much more than a girl, she silently reaffirmed the vow she'd made that she would love him for ever.

'This wasn't the way I wanted to welcome you, baby,' he said wryly. 'But what can I do when I confess I'm an addict for you?' He bent and kissed her, capturing her plump lower lip with his teeth then slowly releasing it as he drew away. 'And I might just die if I don't get my fix.'

In one fluidly effortless movement he suddenly lifted her up high against his chest. Still avidly kissing her, he strode across the honey-coloured wooden floor and headed towards a closed door at the end of it. When they reached the door he kicked it open and carried her across to the palatial black-silk-covered bed that dominated the room. He toed off his shoes and Lara followed suit. And when he drew back the covers and lowered her down onto the sensual silk sheets niceties were forgotten as they tore at each other's clothes and breathlessly dispensed with them.

Their hungry eyes met in mutual wonder just once before Gabriel covered Lara's trembling body with his. And as soon as their skin made contact conversation was rendered redundant. There was simply no need for preamble to the seduction they both longed for.

Gabriel nudged Lara's slim thighs apart with his knee and she immediately sensed her hips soften and then naturally relax. But as she held on tight to the bunched iron biceps in his arms she found herself momentarily tensing as he urgently pushed his hard silken shaft deep inside her. He stilled for a moment. She was more than ready for him, but strangely she felt the eagerly anticipated invasion even more acutely this second time round.

She saw a briefly questioning look in Gabriel's eyes. But the suggestion of uncertainty—if that was what it was—was quickly banished as he started to move deeply inside her, bending his dark head to devour her lips, then her breasts, his searching hands exploring her even as he seduced her.

Yearning to tell him that she loved him, Lara didn't know how she suppressed the impulse. *I'll tell him afterwards*, she vowed, gasping aloud in shock and then pleasure as he bit down on the delicate skin at the juncture of her neck and shoulder with the edges of his teeth.

She couldn't help revelling in the thought that he would be leaving his mark on her in more ways than one. But then she was gasping for a second time when the hot, pulsating need inside her peaked and flooded her with dizzying warmth and she found herself riding an exhilarating wave of pleasure that stole every thought from her head to replace it with unmitigated joy.

The profoundly exquisite experience was heightened when Gabriel suddenly tensed and cried out, spilling his liquid heat deep inside her. His sculpted, handsome face looked to be deeply stunned by the intense release. Lara couldn't help but feel gratified that she had been the one to give him such a gift.

Just before Lara's hot satin heat had enfolded him and he'd driven himself deep inside her Gabriel had shivered hard at the terrifying realisation of how much this woman had come to mean to him. He had been like a cat on a hot tin roof waiting for her to arrive. Not even the demands of the trading floor had been able to distract him from the thought of her for long, and never in his history had he let his guard down so completely around a woman so that she might easily breach it.

He didn't doubt there would be a serious price to pay. But after the stunning satisfaction of their urgent love-making he almost didn't care what that price would be.

'That was amazing,' he breathed, lying down beside her and gathering her against him.

Glancing up, Lara smiled warmly into his eyes. 'I'm glad I wasn't the only one who thought so.' Dropping down again, she pressed her face close to his. 'Gabriel…?'

She whispered his name close against his ear, her soft lips brushing the tender lobe and sending a flurry of goosebumps scudding across his flesh.

'What is it, baby?' He lifted his head to examine her. When he saw that her sultry dark eyes glimmered with tears he immediately tensed. 'What's wrong?'

'Nothing.' Her lips parted in the most engaging and

bewitching smile, and again he was caught off-guard by her incandescent beauty—so much so that his heart *hurt* just looking at her.

'I just want you to know that I'm so glad I waited,' she said gently.

'Waited? For what, sweetheart?'

'To make love with the only man I've ever loved and to give him my virginity.'

If she had struck him hard Gabriel couldn't have been more shocked. He ached for her, body and soul, but somehow right then he found himself immobilised by the confession.

Lara had been a *virgin* when they'd first made love? It didn't make sense. She'd been so willing and ready. Even as doubt settled in the pit of his stomach and seriously unnerved him he remembered that when he'd first taken her she had indeed been exquisitely tight—not at all like an experienced woman...a woman used to having lovers.

In the throes of his passion he had stupidly dismissed the fact. However, he'd thought about it again just now, when they'd made love again.

But what had him reeling even more was Lara's declaration that she loved him—that he was the *only* man she had ever loved. Gabriel honestly didn't know how he felt about that. Love was not something he had ever figured as coming into the equation.

Clearly there was a red-hot attraction between them, but not *love*...surely? Besides, what could a relationship with him bring her other than more grief and pain? She deserved a man who was utterly devoted to her happiness, a man who was whole in every respect of the word, not some embittered automaton that just went through the motions of life but didn't truly enjoy anything very much.

As the waves of shock and surprise and, yes, *fear* continued to eddy through him, Gabriel expelled a long breath in a bid to try and regain his equilibrium. Then he lifted himself away from the lovely woman at his side to lie back against the bank of satin pillows behind them. Glimpsing the confusion in her eyes as he moved away, he felt his heart drum hard as he tried to think what to say to reassure her.

Sitting up, Lara lightly shook her head and folded her arms over her breasts. As she turned to face him he saw the silken skein of long, dark hair that nestled against her collarbone and he longed to give in to the impulse to wind it round his fingers as he had done once before, when things between them had been far less complicated than they suddenly seemed to be.

'Did I—did I say something wrong, Gabriel? Something you didn't like?' she enquired hesitantly.

'You told me that you were on the pill,' he replied, endeavouring to keep his voice steady. No easy feat when his whole world had just been tilted on its head once more.

'It's true. I am. But why should that disturb you? Was it because you thought I must have had other lovers before you?'

'Frankly, yes. I *did* think that.'

'But—but couldn't you tell when you— When we...' Her cheeks reddening, Lara stared at him as if his answer was hard to comprehend.

Emitting a heavy sigh, Gabriel sat up. 'I seem to recall I was driven by lust and desire at the time and wasn't exactly thinking straight. But tell me this, Lara.

If it's true that you were a virgin then why in God's name are you on the pill?'

She drew up her legs beneath the covers and folded her arms round them. 'I take the pill to help regulate my periods. A lot of women do.'

'And you've never slept with another man before me?'

'No.' Her dark eyes flashed. 'I haven't. I don't tell lies, Gabriel.'

'No. Of course you don't. How *could* you, coming from the family that you do?'

It was a back-handed compliment and he wasn't proud of it. Lara had flinched when he'd delivered it. But things between them seemed suddenly to have gained a momentum he hadn't envisaged, and his instinct was to perhaps put the brakes on a little in order to have some time to reflect.

She'd given her virginity to him and told him that she loved him. Whilst both acts were significant in their own way, and had definitely pleased him, did it mean that she was hoping they could make their relationship more permanent? Right at that moment Gabriel didn't see how such a thing could possibly be achieved. How could it when both their lives and their lifestyles were poles apart? As much as he wanted to be with Lara, he couldn't see her taking to life in New York. As beautiful and intelligent as she was, she was more hometown girl than ambitious career woman, and he didn't deny he liked it that she was that way.

Moving across to the edge of the bed as he wrestled with what to do, he reached down for the black silk boxers that, in his haste to make love to Lara, he'd thrown

onto the floor. Hastily pulling them on, he turned back
to survey her and saw her shiver.

Despising himself for not being able to summon
up the words that might help ease her distress, he remarked, 'You should probably get dressed.' Jerking his
head towards another door, he continued, 'You can get a
shower, then come and join me in the living room. You
should find everything you need. I'll use the bathroom
down the hall. We don't have much time before I have
to get back to work and I need to tell you a few things.'

CHAPTER NINE

WHAT THINGS DID HE need to tell her? Lara wondered. She was sure that whatever it was it couldn't possibly bring more distress than she felt already.

Her heart bled because Gabriel hadn't exhibited the slightest pleasure or even *concern* that she'd been a virgin when they'd first made love. In fact he had sounded quite angry about it. Neither had he looked remotely pleased when she'd confessed that she loved him.

Was he really as cold-hearted and uncaring as all that? What if she had made the most horrendous mistake in confessing her feelings to him? She surely hadn't forgotten that he'd rejected her advances once before, albeit a long time ago. But it chilled Lara's blood as she contemplated that perhaps Gabriel really *couldn't* commit to her, or allow himself to love her.

She knew there was a genuinely good man behind those ice-blue eyes, even if the evidence was far too rare, but he was like a wounded bear that snapped at anyone who exhibited concern or ventured too near and she knew the reason why. His fractured—and some might say, dysfunctional—past haunted him. That was why he found kindness and concern so difficult to deal with. Maybe that was also the reason he couldn't immediately accept that she loved him or that she'd given her virginity to *him* rather than another man?

With that unhappy conclusion dominating her thoughts she hastily showered and dressed in the luxurious Art Deco bathroom, reapplied the lipstick that she kept in the pocket of her dress and went in search of the living room to find him.

Promising herself that she would play it cool and not let him see that he had hurt her, nonetheless she felt her heart skip an anxious beat when she saw him again. Gabriel was relaxing on one of the sleek black couches in the light and airy living room with its arresting clear-glassed views of the New York skyline. He had changed into another stylish Italian suit.

The far from welcoming expression on his hard-jawed visage made her insides plunge.

Standing in the doorway, she anxiously smoothed her hand down over the blue tunic dress she'd admired and bought especially for her trip to see him and made a silent vow never to wear it again. In her mind it was jinxed. Moistening her lips, she gave him a greeting that was understandably cautious. From now on she wasn't going to presume anything.

'You said you had some things that you needed to tell me?'

'Why don't you come over here and sit down?' he invited.

Lara thought she spied the merest glimmer of a smile on his lips, but because she wasn't sure she didn't allow herself to believe it. As yet she had no idea what he was going to tell her and couldn't help but fear the worst.

'Did you find everything you needed?' he asked.

'In the bathroom, you mean?'

Gabriel nodded.

'Yes, I did.'

She walked towards him, twisting her hands nervously together in front of her, then stopped, feeling her body helplessly warming when she remembered what they'd been doing just a short while ago. Who could have believed that such heated passion could turn cold so quickly? Gabriel had poured ice water on her feelings when he'd so hastily left her alone in his bed. What if he'd come to the conclusion that she should leave? That he'd made a mistake in inviting her to New York?

Sick with apprehension, she asked, 'Is my suitcase still out in the hall?'

'I've put it in the guest bedroom for now. Later on, when I return from work, I'll take it into my room.'

Even as relief washed through her Lara couldn't help feeling it wasn't right he should have everything his way. 'There's no need.' Lifting her chin, she defied him to disagree with her.

Making her knees knock together, Gabriel rose to his impressive height and covered the space between them. Just bare inches away from her, the scent of his arresting, sexy cologne sent Lara's pulse nervously skittering. Her tender nipples still stung from his attentions in bed, and as she came face to face with him again they burned and tingled fiercely.

'I know I might not be able to give you what you want, Lara,' he said, gravel-voiced. 'But I haven't brought you to New York for us to sleep in separate rooms. I should have been more thoughtful, more caring when we were together just now, but what you told me robbed me of all ability to think straight. I've been reflecting on things and I want to make amends.'

'And how do you plan on doing that? By buying me things? By showing me a good time as is probably your style with the women in your life before you kiss them goodbye and move on to the next one?' Despite her vow not to let him see that he'd upset her, Lara couldn't suppress the scalding angry tears that burned at the backs of her lids. She impatiently wiped them away. 'To be honest, I'd rather go home.'

'No. I don't want that.' A perturbed muscle flinched in the side of his hollowed cheek. 'I want you to stay. Whatever you think of me.'

'Why should it always be about what *you* want, Gabriel? Don't you think that I have needs, too?'

About to turn away, Lara choked back a gasp when she suddenly found herself slammed against his chest and her lips taken prisoner by a hard, hot, almost punishing kiss. Her resolve to leave melted like ice cream beneath the burning rays of a Sahara sun.

As the kiss eased in intensity to become surprisingly tender, Gabriel lifted his head to study her.

'I want you to have what you want, Lara, I really do. But while you're with me I'm afraid I'm driven to be greedy. Perhaps I can't quite believe that you'd surrender your virginity to a man who's notoriously selfish, who puts himself above everyone else when it comes to getting the thing he wants and consequently doesn't consider feelings. But I'm too enamoured of you not to see it as the most unbelievable blessing that you're here, and I can't help but want to make the most of it.'

Reaching out, he cupped the side of her face and looked to be aiming for a smile, but he didn't quite manage it.

'Don't go. Please don't go.'

Lara caught her breath. It wasn't just the simmering desire she saw reflected in his eyes that took her aback, but the almost childlike need that told her he would be nothing less than devastated should she insist on leaving. It was then that she was poignantly reminded that he'd grown up bereft of his mother's love and care, and likely believed he didn't deserve similar consideration from any woman who came into his life.

Moistening lips that still throbbed from his ravenous kisses she carefully examined his carved features. 'I'm not going to leave, Gabriel.' She breathed out a gentle sigh. 'I wouldn't walk out on you when I've given you my word that I'll stay—at least until my holiday comes to an end.'

Seeing the relief that spread across his handsome features, Lara was pleased that he seemed to be reassured.

Recovering her good humour, she teased, 'Besides, do you really think I've come all the way out to New York not to see some of the sights while I'm here?'

'I'll make sure you get to see everything you want to, I swear. Just say the word and I'll arrange it.' His hands dropped to her shoulders. 'And, by the way, one of the things I needed to tell you was that we're going out tonight to a function. It's a corporate dinner at a restaurant not far from the Stock Exchange. I can't duck out of it, I'm afraid. I have to go and I want to take you as my escort.'

It was on the tip of Lara's tongue to say no. She would be so far out of her comfort zone in such elite company and in surroundings that were about as alien to her as the grand Regency house where Gabriel had grown up that it would be no joke. But then she saw the hint of steel in his eyes that told her it would be a waste of time even attempting to refuse, because one way or another he would persuade her differently.

He had never felt more possessive of a woman than when he walked into that stylish New York bar and restaurant with Lara. From the moment they'd arrived heads had turned—not just to greet him, because Gabriel knew everybody who was *anybody*, but to cast curious, admiring glances at his companion. And how could he blame them when Lara added a whole other level to the term 'drop-dead gorgeous'?

The little black dress that she'd insisted was the only suitable garment she'd brought with her to wear to a 'posh' dinner made Gabriel feel like the mythical Ares worshipping at the feet of Aphrodite. It didn't cling to her sublime curves but it couldn't help but pay homage to them whenever she moved. And the way that she wore her hair, in a very feminine loose topknot, with curling tendrils brushing the sides of her cheeks, and with her shoulders bare courtesy of the halterneck style of the dress, she looked utterly exquisite.

Gabriel's hand gripped Lara's a little tighter as they moved through the crowd milling around the bar. There were more greetings and back-slapping as people recognised him, and frankly for once he could have done without it.

When he sensed that his companion was drawing back, and guessed she was feeling overwhelmed, he deliberately pulled her near and his smile was reassuring. She wasn't used to this. The stylishly attired Wall Street patrons and the competitive atmosphere they created whenever they were together was a million light years away from the world Lara inhabited.

Although the air was drenched with the smell of alluring perfume and expensive cologne, the predominant scent was that of money. It was strange how the realisation didn't give Gabriel his usual sense of pleasure or the satisfaction that he'd grown to depend on.

Looking for an out, he caught the eye of the maître d' and asked him to show them into the private dining room where they were scheduled to eat.

The gathering had been set up in one of the most intimately sophisticated rooms of the restaurant which was frequently the chosen venue for the private meetings he had with his executive clientele. But tonight Gabriel's fellow guests would be some of the key players who had worked with him to help avert yet another serious financial crisis. After the tough few weeks they had endured, and the intense few days when it had been touch and go and Gabriel had been called in to join them, they would be in the mood to celebrate. Although by no means could anyone rest on their laurels yet.

The effusive greetings of his fellow diners over, Gabriel was relieved to be able to sit down next to Lara and look at the menu. It didn't escape his notice that her slender fingers shook slightly as she perused what was on offer, and neither did he miss her soft-voiced sigh. His broad-suited shoulder brushed against hers as he leant towards her and he caught the faint but arousing scent of her honeyed perfume. His stomach clenched hard with desire.

Lowering his voice he asked, 'How are you bearing up? I promise this won't go on for too long.'

His reward was a too brief glimpse of a smile.

'I'm all right. I think.'

Gabriel's own smile was more generous. 'I can't

say that *I* am. I'd much rather we were alone together than here at this dinner,' he confessed. 'And, trust me, I wouldn't be here at all if I had the choice.'

It was impossible to suppress the need and desire that crept into his tone. In truth, it was hard even to think straight when Lara was around.

'I'm bowled over by the fact that you're actually here,' he went on, 'and that you came all this way just to see me. By the way, this is a very good menu. "Bankers' fare", they call it. If you want a recommendation, can I suggest the filet mignon?'

Unable to resist, he let his avid gaze into her sultry brown eyes deliberately linger, quite aware that there was running speculation round the table about their relationship. After all, Lara was an unknown entity to them. A very beautiful and desirable unknown entity.

Before she could comment on his suggestion of cuisine, one of the top city bankers across the table—a man called Lars Jensen—leaned towards them and asked confidently, 'So, Lara—can I call you that?— I'm intrigued, as all my colleagues are. How did you meet Gabriel? He has a reputation of being a bit of a wizard here on Wall Street—a regular Croesus. Whatever he touches turns to gold. Did you perhaps have some business dealings with him in London? If you did, lucky you.'

The suited young man seated opposite her, with his fashionable, close-cut fair hair and too-inquisitive green eyes, had honed in on Lara like a missile poised to attack. Having no idea how much or how little Gabriel wanted her to reveal, she made her quietly voiced response carefully measured.

'I know nothing about the financial world and, no,

we didn't meet in London. Gabriel went to university with my brother. That's how we met.'

'I'm even more intrigued. You mean that you've known him all these years and he hasn't mentioned you? At least not in my hearing.'

'Why should he mention me? We're just friends.'

Catching an expression that was almost a glower on Gabriel's handsome face, Lara sensed herself flush. Had she said the wrong thing? What else could she have said? That she was an ex-girlfriend of his? That patently wasn't true.

'So you're "just friends", are you?' Lars's tone was mockingly doubtful as his laserlike glance pinioned them both. 'Is that a new euphemism for lovers in the UK?'

'No, it isn't,' Gabriel interjected firmly, his hard jaw clenching. Out of sight, his hand folded possessively over Lara's. 'And if I tell you that Lara was only six-teen when we first met, I doubt you'd think we would have been lovers, would you?'

This time the other man's searching gaze lingered over-long on Lara, making a mental inventory of her assets almost as if she was some kind of lucrative deal he was convinced would add to his fortune.

Lowering his voice, he briefly turned his attention back to Gabriel, commenting, 'Don't tell me you weren't tempted?'

Beside her, Lara intimately sensed the silent fury and tension in her companion's body as if it were her own.

'I think we should drop the subject. don't you? Lara is my guest here and your inappropriate insinuations are making her uncomfortable. That's not acceptable.'

His ice-blue gaze swept the table. 'And that goes for all of you.'

There was a sudden marked silence and Lara wanted the floor to open up and swallow her. If anything Gabriel's warning had only increased the curiosity in the other guests' eyes. Squeezing his hand to get his attention, she felt her heart thump hard when she immediately got it. His eyes shot little sparks of tangible electricity at her.

'What is it?' he demanded.

'You don't have to defend me. I'm sure your friend didn't mean anything by what he said.'

'You know that for sure, do you?' Tugging her towards him, so that what he said would be for her ears and her ears only, he whispered, 'Number one, he's not a friend—he's a colleague, and a very ambitious and ruthless colleague. You should be aware that we're sitting at a table full of hungry sharks, my angel, and right now *you're* the bait.'

Lara shivered. As her eyes strayed across the table to the rest of the glittering company, clad in their perfect Italian suits and breathtaking haute couture, she was stunned to realise that everyone was examining her and trying to figure out exactly who she was, as if it wasn't a usual occurrence for Gabriel to bring an unknown woman to these functions with him.

Feeling her face flame self-consciously at being the centre of so much attention, she turned back to her companion. 'I need to go to the ladies' room,' she murmured.

Gabriel immediately signalled to a nearby waitress and asked her to direct her. But as he stood back and helped her to her feet Lara sensed his reluctance and frustration at having to release her even for a second.

* * *

Lara felt as if she deserved a prize for enduring one of the most discomfiting and tense evenings of her life. But at the end of it one thing was absolutely clear. What she'd witnessed of the superficial and pressured life of the New York financial 'elite' wasn't for her.

Even though it was a dream come true to be with Gabriel, she was already longing to return home to the simple yet satisfying day-to-day routine she was familiar with—a way of life where she didn't have to be overly concerned about what people thought of her or whether she was wearing the right outfit to go to dinner or to work. Even at the college library she could get away with wearing jeans and a T-shirt.

That said, Gabriel looked nothing less than *edible* in his flawless Italian tailoring. One of the female guests at their table had obviously deliberately followed her out to the loo, and had blatantly quizzed her about her relationship with him. When Lara had frostily declined to tell her, the other woman had immediately shared a 'no-holds barred' graphic illustration of what she'd personally like to do with him in bed.

Lara's jaw had dropped at the woman's sheer temerity. It was obvious that Gabriel's warning to his assembled peers not to make her feel unduly uncomfortable was only to be adhered to as they sat round the dinner table. Out of his sight it was open season for the sharks to feed. Lara had quickly discovered that going to the dinner as Gabriel's guest didn't automatically grant her immunity from the other women who desired him and wouldn't hesitate to tell her so.

It was a relief to return to the apartment, even though Gabriel had been broodingly quiet on the journey home.

Inevitably her anxiety had been building because of his lack of communication, and as soon as they were alone again Lara immediately turned to him for some answers as to the reason why.

'What's wrong?' she asked as he shrugged off his suit jacket and hung it on the steel coat stand inside the door. 'I get the feeling that you're unhappy. Didn't you enjoy the dinner? Your colleagues were certainly glad to see you.'

He curled his lip. 'It may come as a surprise to you, Lara, but on Wall Street it pays to stay on good terms with the boss. With the money, as they say here. If you think that people were glad to see me simply because they love my company then you're more naïve than I thought.'

Toeing off her shoes, as was her habit when she was at home, Lara heaved an annoyed sigh.

'Do you get off on cutting me down to size, Gabriel? Does it stroke your ego to do that? Obviously it must. And anyway why *shouldn't* people be glad of your company? You can be quite pleasant when you try, though I confess that's not very—'

The final word of her little speech was unceremoniously cut off as Gabriel hauled her against his chest and devoured her lips with a hard, open-mouthed kiss. As soon as his silken tongue drove into her mouth and his hands moved down her body to lift up her skirt and touch her intimately Lara felt immediately and frighteningly powerless to deny him anything. It appalled her that she couldn't even put up a fight. But then why would she want to, she reasoned, when she loved him so much that it hurt?

'Right now I can't take it slowly,' he breathed hotly

against her mouth. 'I confess you've become irresistible to me, and I can't take it slowly because I want you
too much, but afterwards...'

Lara momentarily held her breath as she sensed his
hand slide into her panties. When his searching fingers invaded her and pushed up she gasped, her head
falling against his hard-muscled shoulder. Her senses
were instantly drowned by the heat from his body and
the seductive, sultry scent of his masculine cologne. If
he hadn't been holding her she might easily have sunk
down to the floor, because her limbs were rendered
weak as a kitten's.

'Afterwards,' he continued, his free hand caressing
the back of her neck, 'we'll take it nice and slow and
really get to know each other, find out what gives us
the most pleasure.'

Unable to reply because she was suddenly swept
away on a sea of delectation so profoundly erotic that
she couldn't speak, Lara pressed her cheek against Gabriel's pristine white shirt, registering the wild beating of his heart against her ear and wondering what
she could do to make him feel similarly swept away.

She hardly seemed to know herself when she was
with this man. All she could think about in his company was fulfilling her most carnal desires and hopefully fulfilling his, too. Had her self-enforced celibacy
all these years turned her into some kind of insatiable siren?

When she lifted her head it was to find Gabriel staring down at her with an intensity that almost stopped
her heart. 'What you do to me...' she murmured softly,
tenderly touching her hand to his cheek.

His piercing blue eyes crinkling in acknowledgement, he lifted her up into his arms as though her weight didn't even signify. Then, still holding her gaze he affirmed huskily, 'We need to go to bed. *Now.*'

CHAPTER TEN

THE FOLLOWING WEEK passed like the most fantastical dream. Whilst her days were spent sightseeing and touring the city—courtesy of Barry, Gabriel's attentive chauffeur—Lara's nights were all given over to Gabriel. On occasion he wined and dined her at wonderful restaurants, took her to the cinema or to see a show on Broadway, but whatever the entertainment or pleasure they participated in, the high point of every evening was always when they returned to Gabriel's apartment and to each other's arms.

Knowing that her short holiday was quickly coming to an end, and that soon she would be going home to England to resume her post as college librarian, Lara started to feel painfully anxious about the future of her relationship with Gabriel. Did they even *have* a future together? They had a powerful connection, certainly, and there was no disputing the fact that she loved him, but as he had noticeably avoided discussing commitment and making their association more meaningful, Lara couldn't help but be apprehensive.

She had seen first-hand how devoted he was to what he did, and how seductive it must be to be so highly regarded in the financial arena he worked in. His colleagues all seemed to view Gabriel as practically irreplaceable. But did that mean he would never consider returning to the UK and once more making it his home?

During the time Lara had spent with him in New York he had never even mentioned the family home that he'd inherited. She was wary of trying to get him to discuss it in case it stirred up the fury and despair he'd expressed when he'd read his uncle's letter, yet she knew that Gabriel would never come to terms with what had happened and start to heal his past if he never even addressed the issue.

What did he intend to do about the Regency manor house that he'd grown up in? Did he plan to sell it and not even consider going back to reside there?

If that were the case, and he stayed in New York, Lara was pretty certain she wouldn't be joining him. The elite, sophisticated lifestyle and relentlessly driven aims of the bankers and financiers to make and acquire even more money and kudos epitomised everything she and her family disliked about the pursuit of material success in the world. As her brother, Sean, used to say, 'What good is being rich if you don't do something good with your wealth to help those less privileged on the planet?'

But Lara's dilemma was more than just the fact that that particular way of living didn't chime with her personal values. It had much more to do with her despair that Gabriel had never even once told her that he loved her. She had begun to suspect that he never would. Already she feared their heated, passionate union would be very quickly put aside to be replaced by even more work demands and perhaps occasionally the company of one of those 'pretty ladies' he'd mentioned that he called upon whenever he got lonely.

Was she really so hard to love? And would he honestly prefer that lonely and ultimately empty existence over enjoying Lara's love and devotion for the rest of his life? Not to mention the possibility of creating a family of their own....

Sipping at a glass of orange juice in the living room as she waited for him to reappear that evening—he'd got back late from work and was still getting ready so that they could go out to dinner—Lara stared out at the stunning New York skyline of silver and shadows and felt unbearably sad.

Her sojourn here was rapidly coming to an end, and as yet nothing had been resolved between them about their relationship. This was to be her last night in the city because tomorrow she was flying home, and so far, aside from giving her the details of her flight, Gabriel had hardly even mentioned it.

'Hey.'

The smoky cadence of his voice had her turning quickly, and just in time she managed to avoid spilling juice all over the pretty midnight blue silk dress Gabriel had bought her.

She had never sought for him to buy her gifts, and had frequently told him so whenever he suggested it, but when he'd told her he'd stepped out of his office one afternoon to visit a high-end store so that he might get her 'something pretty to wear to dinner', Lara had been helplessly touched by his thoughtfulness. Pleased, too. The garment was sleek and fitted, and when she'd taken it out of the stylish carrier bag and unwrapped it from its carefully folded tissue paper she'd been taken aback at just how perfect it was.

She shouldn't have been surprised that it fitted as though made for her, because her lover had an astute eye for the details that many men might miss—not to mention intimately knowing the lines and curves of her body. The thought that he'd committed them to memory made her blood throb and heat in anticipation of the next time they would make love.

Setting the tall glass of juice aside, she curved her lips in an affectionate smile of awe and admiration. Gabriel stood before her dressed in another flawless suit, combined with a navy silk shirt and sky blue tie. His chestnut hair was swept back off his face to reveal the carved, clean lines that she was sure Michelangelo himself would have hungered to paint or sculpt.

'Hey, yourself.'

'I see you're wearing the dress…. Stand up—let me see how it fits.'

Getting to her feet, Lara obligingly made a slow turn to show off the dress from every angle.

An array of tumultuous feelings hit Gabriel all at once. But first and foremost was the dizzying sensation of warmth that flooded his heart—flooded it like a cascading waterfall where, if you were to stand underneath it, you would scarcely be able to draw breath with the force of it.

As he stood and surveyed the bewitching combination of beauty and sensuality that was Lara, and sensed his blood start to pound with the inevitable hunger and need that always arose when she was near, he wondered if that alien feeling was love. That sense of complete and utter helplessness in the face of something that he'd always told himself he didn't want? That hitching of his heart and the weakness in his limbs whenever he caught sight of the woman he intuitively knew he would be willing to *die* for in order to keep safe? And—more than that—the feeling of devastating loss he imagined he would suffer if he were never to see her again? Surely they were all signs that pointed to him being head over heels in love with Lara?

But what followed that wondrous revelation was the dark demon of fear. Fear that he might ruin her life because he had no experience of caring for such a priceless jewel.

For so long Gabriel had held himself apart from any sensitivity or feeling around women in case he got hurt. Look what his own mother had done to him. With such a precarious introduction into the world, trust—particularly when it came to women—was surely going to be an ongoing issue for him.

His thinking ran along the lines of what if he allowed himself to get involved with someone and then got hurt so badly he would never be able to recover enough to do the one thing that he did well? That was acquiring money and status in his chosen field. At least that gave him options with regard to how he lived. And in any case, surely it was better to be rich and miserable rather than the reverse?

Mentally giving himself a shake, Gabriel turned his attention back to the dress Lara was modelling. It could indeed have been tailor-made for her exquisite form— and, being personally acquainted with just *how* exquisite that form was, he knew, with a glimmer of pride, that he had chosen so well.

'You look utterly beautiful—in fact, you're ravish-ing,' he told her.

'It's the dress.'

'Can't you accept a compliment for once without put-ting yourself down, for goodness' sake?'

As soon as the words left his lips Gabriel wanted to take them back. His thoughtless remark had made Lara's cheeks flush with embarrassed heat and he was once again reminded of his fears around loving her. In truth, he couldn't bear the idea of hurting her even *once*, let alone the many times he might thoughtlessly hurt her should they spend the rest of their lives together.

Tucking her hair behind an ear, she lifted her shoul-ders in a shrug. 'Perhaps I'm not very good at receiving compliments—which is why I try and deflect them with humour. It doesn't mean that I don't appreciate you say-ing nice things to me, Gabriel. What woman *wouldn't* want a man to tell her she looks beautiful?'

'I'm sorry I snapped at you. I guess I'm just feeling a little on edge, knowing that you're leaving tomorrow,' he admitted, his chest tightening at the thought. He went to her then and folded her into his arms. Resting his chin on the top of her head, he stroked his hand down her back and immediately sensed her quiver. 'I should kidnap you and stop you from going,' he murmured.

Moving back a little, so that she might examine him, Lara knew her luminous brown eyes couldn't hide her disquiet.

'You don't have to resort to kidnapping me to get me to stay with you, Gabriel. I'd gladly stay with you if you just simply asked.' She sighed and shook her head. 'But you *won't*, will you? Just simply ask, I mean?'

She was beginning to know him too well. 'Aren't

you looking forward to going back to England—to your family and your job…your life there?' he replied, hoping to divert her.

'Of course I am. Can I ask you something?'

Her voice had lowered softly and he guessed she was wary of upsetting him. He hated the idea that Lara felt she had to walk on eggshells around him.

Releasing her, he restlessly drove his fingers through his hair. 'What is it you want to ask?'

'Have you… Have you ever thought of coming back to England to settle? I mean, what about the house that you inherited from your family? Have you made up your mind about what you're going to do with it?'

'Yes, I have. I'll be travelling back in a few days to sign some papers. I'm sorry I didn't tell you before, but it just never seemed to be the appropriate time.'

'You're selling it, aren't you? That means you won't be coming back to settle, doesn't it?'

Gabriel swallowed hard. It was time to tell Lara the truth—the *whole* truth.

'In my uncle's letter, he stipulated that I could only inherit if I came back to live in the manor for at least six months. After that I could do what I liked with the house.'

Her eyes lit up and he saw the hope that flared in their silken depths.

'Then you *could* come back to live there? We could see each other whenever we wanted?'

'Sweetheart, as difficult as it might be for you to understand, I don't want to live in that house again. It holds too many unhappy memories for me. I'd be much better off selling it and staying here.'

The colour drained from Lara's face. 'But didn't you

just say that your uncle stipulated in his letter that you
could only inherit if you lived there for six months? If
you're not planning on doing that, how will you sell it?
It won't be yours to sell, will it?'

'I have a very good lawyer. There are ways and
means to get round the legalities.'

'I don't understand….'

Her voice faltered a little and she looked as if she
might cry. Gabriel felt like the worst criminal.

'I mean, it's not as though you need the money, is it?
Why not just keep the house? Keep it for your family?'

He stared at her. 'You know I don't have any family.' He ground out the words as if they might choke
him. What was Lara playing at, coming out with such
a thing?

'I mean that you might one day have a family of your
own. That would help dispel the unhappy memories of
living in the house, wouldn't it?'

'I'm happy to take risks in my working life, Lara,
but not in my personal one. Don't you know that by
now?'

He saw her take a nervous swallow, then slide her
palms down over the pretty blue dress he'd bought her.
She lifted her shimmering gaze to his.

'I suppose I do. I just hoped that, given time, you'd
come to see things differently. The eternal optimist—
that's me.' Her lips quirked in a self-deprecating smile.
'Shouldn't we go to dinner now? It's getting late, and I
ought to try and get a good night's sleep before travelling tomorrow. I'll just go and get my jacket.'

As Lara left the room, Gabriel stared blankly ahead
of him out of the window at the winking lights of the
city that had helped him to make his fortune. And

right then he despised himself and *it* for contributing to breaking the heart of one of the sweetest and loveliest women in the world....

They sat down on their last night together to what should have been a wonderful meal at a local Thai restaurant, but for Lara the delicious food might as well have been gruel for all the enjoyment it gave her.

She was numb from her head down to her toes. The realisation that Gabriel wasn't any nearer to changing his mind about returning to England to face the demons from his past or to consider the possibility of committing to a proper relationship with her had finally sunk in. He'd asserted that he was happy to take risks in his working life but not in his personal one. The declaration had shattered her heart because she knew it was the death knell to all her hopes and dreams where he was concerned. What else could she do now but accept his decision to continue living his life in New York without her?

'Don't you like the food I ordered for you?' As he laid his fork down by the side of his plate, Gabriel's lean, hollow-cheeked face was grim. He reached up to loosen his tie as if he suddenly couldn't bear the constriction.

Biting back the tears that precariously threatened, Lara dabbed at her lips with her napkin. 'I know you meant well, bringing me here to eat, but I'm afraid I don't have much of an appetite.'

'You should have said.'

'I didn't because you've been working all day and I didn't have anything at the apartment to cook for you. I knew you needed to eat. That's why I agreed to go out to dinner with you.'

'As usual, putting others before yourself.' Although he'd lowered his voice, the muted volume didn't disguise the disparagement in his tone.

Lara flinched. 'You make it sound like it's something you despise—to think of others, I mean. I can't help my nature, Gabriel.'

His blue eyes were as clear and cold as flawless diamonds. 'No, you can't, can you? That's why I knew it was probably a mistake to start this affair. But I'm only human and I simply couldn't resist.'

If she hadn't been trembling so hard at his words, and feared losing her balance should she attempt to stand, Lara knew she couldn't have remained sitting in her seat. For the first time ever she honestly felt she disliked the man who gazed back at her across the table.

'Is that really all you thought us being together was? An affair? Something you could take or leave? I knew you had the potential to be cruel, Gabriel, but I never guessed just *how* cruel.'

'Why? It isn't as though I haven't given you enough evidence.'

'You're right. You started giving me evidence all those years ago, when I was just sixteen.'

Lara's comment drew a disturbed frown between Gabriel's brows. 'When you were sixteen? I doubt it. You surely didn't take it seriously when I used to rib you about not having a boyfriend because you were so choosy?'

'It wasn't that. Don't you remember Sean's party? The one he threw at our house? I know you do because you talked about it that first day, when you showed up to offer your condolences for Sean. Well, that night you were flirting with me, and in my innocence I took it to

mean that you liked me. I mean *really* liked me. I foolishly told you how I felt about you....'

Lara paused. The memory was suddenly more acute
than it had ever been. The power of it made her ribs
hurt.

'I don't think it pleased you. If anything, you were
probably highly embarrassed. You told me I should look
to be with someone my own age. Then you saw that
blonde tutor from your university across the room and
you all but pushed me aside to get to her. So yes, Gabriel. I *do* know that you can be cruel.'

He shook his head. 'That was a long time ago. You
were just a kid. I wouldn't have wanted to encourage
your interest because you were my best friend's little
sister and your family's regard was important to me.'

'But feelings are feelings, no matter what age you
are, and even then mine ran deep, Gabriel. Anyway,
we're talking about what's happening *now*. What I
want to know is are you reducing what we have to the
description of a mere affair because you're trying to
protect yourself from being hurt should you commit
seriously to me? I don't understand. How can I hurt
you if you don't really let me into your life, Gabriel?'

'As hard as it might be for you to hear, Lara, I don't
need anyone in my life. My life is just fine the way it is.'

'Is that true?' Sadly shaking her head, Lara barely
knew how to proceed. Gabriel was implacable when he
erected his defences. As hard as iron. She knew that.

'It's pointless continuing this conversation.' Throwing down his napkin, he signalled for the waiter. 'I'll
only hurt you even more if we continue, and you're
going home tomorrow.'

Lara stayed in her seat and said softly, 'You're probably right. Okay. Why don't you just pay the bill and we'll go?'

'Wise decision,' he murmured, just at the same moment as the smiling waiter arrived at their table.

It truly amazed Lara how quickly she had got back into the routine of working after the long summer break. In the endless days and long, sleepless nights following her departure from Gabriel in New York she'd wondered if she'd ever find pleasure or satisfaction in the job she loved again. But as soon as she had returned to the college, and the requests and demands of the students for help with their research, she'd taken both refuge and pleasure in the familiar routine of the life she was used to.

It helped her not to dwell on Gabriel too much. She would have been utterly useless doing her job if she had.

Yet the memory of their agonising goodbye at the airport and his comment that he'd known it was a mistake to start their affair still had the power to make her cry.

The distance he'd put between them at the restaurant with his remark the night before she was due to leave had grown even wider when he'd told her he thought it best they slept in separate rooms, so that Lara could get a good night's rest before catching her flight the next day. Even though he'd been hateful at the restaurant she hadn't slept a wink. Without Gabriel in the bed next to her—the Gabriel who had been so loving and passionate—she'd felt as if an essential part of her was missing.

Although she'd told herself she didn't understand his sudden cold impulse to distance himself from her not just physically but emotionally, in truth she did understand. He'd been running away again. Not just from

Lara, but from his fear of love and all that that might mean. He simply didn't trust it in case it was taken away, just as his mother had been taken away from him when she took her own life. That was why he'd taunted Lara with his remark that their 'affair' had been a mistake. He'd been trying to push her away. He wouldn't run the risk of caring for her too much in case she ended up hurting him.

The next morning, although they'd sat at the dining table together for breakfast, Gabriel had busied himself making several calls on his cell phone that had ensured his attention was on his work and not on her.

Lara might as well have been invisible. She'd tried hard to make conversation, hoping to engage him with her heartfelt declaration that she was still going to miss him despite what he had said at the restaurant, and that it would be hard to go home knowing they might not ever see each other again.

Gabriel's handsome face had remained worryingly impassive, as though he was deliberately locking her out—locking her out of his mind and his heart—and finally, when his chauffeur had called to tell him the car was ready to take them to the airport, out of his life, too.

When he'd left her at the airport he'd hesitatingly laid his hands on her shoulders and bent his head to kiss her. Lara had tensed helplessly, hoping and praying that he was going to have a change of heart and declare he couldn't just let her disappear out of his life without making some plans for the future. But to add to her distress his parting kiss hadn't been the least bit passionate or heartfelt. They might have just been mere acquaintances. The touch of his lips had been briefly warm and perfunctory, nothing more. Then, after telling her to take care of herself, that he'd probably be in touch just as soon as he 'got his head straight', he'd turned on his heel and hadn't looked back even once as he'd exited the airport.

Back at work, despite her vow not to dwell too much on her longing for Gabriel, memories of his warm, hard body against hers, of the smiles that had tugged at her heart because they were so rare and therefore even more precious, of the sound of his voice especially before he made love to her, when he'd seductively enticed and teased her, would sneak up on her when Lara least expected it. She would wonder what he was doing and if he even gave her a second thought. Had Gabriel already replaced her in his bed with some pretty, ambitious girl who viewed him as a sure-fire ticket to success and fortune? A girl who might please him sexually but would never love him—not like *she* loved him.

'Hello, Miss Bradley. Did you have a good holiday?'

She blinked, then glanced up from the paperwork she'd been desperately trying to apply herself to before thoughts of Gabriel had intruded once again.

A tall, slim young man dressed in skinny jeans and an unironed T-shirt stood on the other side of the counter. He had a shock of sandy-coloured hair in dire need of a wash and a comb. Lara immediately relaxed. Danny Fairfax was one of the most pleasant students you could wish to meet—charming and affable, in spite of his sometimes unkempt appearance. She always made sure to make time for him when he needed help with some aspect of the research he was struggling with.

'It was fine, thanks.' She followed up this answer with an unguarded, warm smile. Danny immediately flushed beetroot-red, which endeared him to her even more. 'And I told you before to call me Lara. "Miss Bradley" makes me sound like some elderly spinster.'

His lips broke into a grin. But he quickly looked serious again. 'I'm sorry I asked if your holiday was good. I forgot that you told me your brother had recently died. Obviously you must still be grieving for him.'

The comment took Lara aback. Not just because Danny had remembered the fact but also because she realised she'd probably been thinking more about Gabriel than about Sean. Of course she still missed her brother's presence, and not a day went by when she didn't mourn him, but Gabriel was a living, breathing reality, and when she'd been with him he had reached deep down inside her and stolen both her heart and her soul. She knew Sean would understand, even give her his blessing. He had loved Gabriel, too.

Staring back into Danny's strangely still grey eyes, Lara wondered if he would ever experience the depth of love and passion that she had experienced with Gabriel. She could only pray that he wouldn't have his heart splintered and broken as hers had been.

'Yes, I'm still grieving. But losing someone like that… It still feels like they're around. You know what I mean? His presence is everywhere.' It didn't pass Lara by that she might have been talking about Gabriel.

'Yes, I do know what you mean,' Danny answered gravely. 'I lost my dad two years ago at Christmas and sometimes I hear his voice as though he's in the room with me, especially when I'm trying to work out a problem. He was from Yorkshire, and when things got tough he always used to say, "Don't let the man grind you down!" Funny how that used to help me.'

'He sounds as though he was a very wise man, your dad.'

'He was. He was the best.'

'So, Danny…' Lara purposefully switched back into work mode. It wouldn't help her to dwell on her personal sorrows too much and nor would it help Danny—although she was touched that he would share the story of his personal loss with her. It was good to know that she wasn't the only one walking around with the feeling that life had pulled the rug from under her and she might never walk on firm ground again. 'What can I do for you today?'

Gabriel had been revisiting his old bedroom. Although his initial reaction on entering it had been wary, his stomach clenched hard in readiness for the deluge of hurtful memory that would inevitably swamp him, he had been mildly surprised to see that the room was newly decorated, freshened up.

Had Richard Devenish undertaken to get a decorator in before he'd fallen ill? Why on earth had he done that? It wasn't as though he'd needed an extra room. Had he perhaps believed that his nephew would return and make the manor his home again?

Bemused, Gabriel allowed his gaze to sweep his surroundings in a preliminary search. His glance falling on the neatly arranged books in the two maplewood bookcases that he remembered from his childhood, he leant down to retrieve a first edition copy of *Brave New World* by Aldous Huxley. It had been a Christmas present from his uncle when he was just nine. He had all but devoured the book. He'd loved it so much he had even written an essay about it at school.

That year his teacher had commented in his report, *'Gabriel is a precocious reader with a highly inventive imagination that I am sure will take him far!'*

His lips nudging a bittersweet smile, he replaced the book and turned round. Janet Mullan, the housekeeper, had left the large picture windows open to let in the sunshine. The scent of stocks and roses from the garden below also drifted in delicately, filling the air with the heady summer perfume that Gabriel had always loved even as a boy.

Releasing a slow, contemplative breath, he walked to the windows to stare out at the stunning vista. He recalled thinking at that time that it wouldn't be so bad living here if he could have a few of the boys from school to come and stay with him in the holidays. But his nanny—a middle-aged lady called Margaret—had shaken her head and reminded him that his uncle had forbidden it, in case any of the valuable antiques in the house got broken.

To make up for his disappointment she'd given him a hug, ruffled his hair and said she'd take him to the local fair on the village green…perhaps he'd see some of his friends there? Well, Gabriel had gone to the fair, munched at a toffee apple and a sticky bun, palled up with a local boy and had a whale of a time, sliding down the helter-skelter and riding the carousel. That had been one of the best days of that summer, he recalled.

But sadly, events like that had been too few and far between. His taciturn uncle had grown more and more distant, seemingly preferring to stay away rather than share the house with Gabriel when he was home, and concepts like heritage and family had quickly grown to mean less and less to his nephew. The next summer holiday that Gabriel had properly enjoyed had been after his first year at university, when he had met Sean.

Inevitably, the thought of his best friend brought with it a new deluge of heartfelt memories—of Lara and the stricken look on her pretty face when he'd bade her goodbye less than warmly at the airport. It had been the hardest thing he'd ever done, and every night and day that had passed since had given him plenty of cause to regret it. It had been a cruel way to end their too-brief relationship—pretending that he didn't care how she felt. It had been the act of his life.

The truth was he cared too much. He just hadn't been able to deal with the outpouring of love and affection that he'd received from Lara. It had been a totally unfamiliar experience to have someone love him and want to be with him—not because of what he could materially provide for them but because they wanted to be with the man behind the facade Gabriel had affected all these years. The *real* Gabriel Devenish.

But why should he let Lara waste her love on him? Sooner or later she'd find out that he just wasn't worth it. In years to come, when she was married to a really decent man, she'd thank him for it.

Feeling an overwhelming sense of weariness and despair descend, he lowered himself onto the bed, put his hands behind his head, and lay down. His uncle's solicitor was waiting for him downstairs in the drawing room—waiting for Gabriel to give him his decision about what he intended to do with the house. Remembering that he'd also promised his property developer friend that he would ring him to discuss some figures regarding the potential sale of the manor, Gabriel loosed a heavy sigh and shut his eyes.

CHAPTER ELEVEN

LARA COULDN'T FATHOM what on earth was wrong with her. Yes, she'd been through the mill, losing first Sean and then Gabriel. But were those heartrending events enough to make her feel queasy and persistently light-headed, which was how she'd been feeling for several days now? She should perhaps go the doctor, but she was sure she would eventually shrug it off so steered clear of pursuing that option. Instead she determinedly focused on work, even putting in some overtime in a bid to shake herself out of whatever was ailing her.

Besides, she wasn't the only one who had lost a loved one or had her heart broken. What she should aim to do was to be more stoical. She should just endeavour to take one day at a time and somehow, some way, garner some optimism about life again.

Then one morning, as she got ready for work, Lara reached into her purse to dig out the foil packet of contraceptive pills. She immediately realised she'd picked up the previous month's packet instead of the current one. About to jettison the empty container into a nearby wicker basket, she did a double take. At the beginning of the empty rows there was one tablet remaining. How had that happened? More to the point, why hadn't she noticed it before?

Her heart started to pound as she calculated back to the week of the remaining pill. Without a doubt it was the week that she'd spent in New York with Gabriel. Six weeks had passed since then. Six weeks with no sign of a period. Lara had put the absence down to the emotional rollercoaster she'd been on, telling herself that everything would sort itself out just as soon as her emotions calmed down.

Hadn't she started to take the pill in the first place to help regulate her periods because they tended to be erratic? She shouldn't be alarmed that she'd missed one. Yet some instinct told her that she *did* perhaps need to be concerned.

Dragging her hand feverishly through her tousled dark hair, and still in her pyjamas, she sat down on the bed and let the realisation that had shockingly dawned wash over her. Wasn't it true that you had to be consistent when taking an oral contraceptive? If you missed one then you risked the inevitable. Suddenly, the reason for her queasiness, her feelings of being light-headed and her missed period became disturbingly clear. She was pregnant. Pregnant with Gabriel Devenish's baby!

It was the strangest thing, but suddenly Lara's sense of confusion and worry about her health dissipated like ice crystals beneath the sun. She would need to take a test to be absolutely sure, of course.... Touching her palm to her cheek, she sensed her skin flush warmly. A sense of joyous excitement filled her. It went racing through her blood like life-giving oxygen.

How or why she had omitted to take one of her pills no longer seemed to matter. She certainly hadn't forgotten to take one deliberately. In any case, Gabriel hadn't got in touch when he'd 'got his head straight', as he'd promised he would. He hadn't even let her know when and if he'd returned to the UK to deal with the sale of his family's manor house.

As much as it grieved her, Lara could no longer make that her driving concern. In her mind and in her heart she had left the door open for him to come back to her— of course she had. But if he didn't—and right now it didn't look as if he would—well, she would have their son or daughter to take care of, and that would in time help to ease the hurt of his desertion.

At least she hoped that it would. But whatever happened one thing was certain: she intended to be the most loving and adoring mother she could be. She might not be wealthy, but her child would be the recipient of far more important riches—her love and devotion. He or she might not have a father in their life, but that would have to be enough.

Gabriel had spent the morning with his architect, perusing and discussing the renovation plans for the manor which were already well under way. The genteel old orangery was being redesigned, along with the bedrooms, and he'd also had discussions with one of Britain's top garden designers about what could be done to make the most of the gardens.

The day the solicitor had visited the house to find out what Gabriel intended to do about it, Gabriel had made the surprising decision to fulfil the terms of the codicil to the will and live there for the six months stipulated so that he could inherit. Shortly after that he had rung his office in New York and told them he was taking a year's sabbatical in order to decide what he wanted to do about his future.

His decision to take a year off had dumbfounded his employers, and they had immediately offered him a myriad of financial temptations and seductive inducements like a prestigious house in the Hamptons to get him to rethink. Gabriel had firmly declined.

The most surprising thing of all was that when he had come off the phone he'd felt as if a huge weight had been lifted off his shoulders. Until that cathartic moment he hadn't fully realised how much his work and his drive for more success, more money and more power had dominated his life. It certainly hadn't left much time or space for anything else. In particular, for the loving and committed relationship he secretly craved but had always feared he would never be able to sustain even if he found it.

During the past few weeks since he had returned to the house and reread his uncle's letter—particularly the part where he had told him of his hopes that he would return to live at the manor and raise his children there—Gabriel had been filled with new hope and optimism about his future. A future quite unlike the usual picture he had envisaged for himself.

What had helped tremendously was the fact that he had actually started to fall in love with the house. Bit by bit the sorrow of his childhood and his damaged past had loosened its grip and he had started to heal.

One afternoon, whilst exploring one of the larger bedrooms which the housekeeper was convinced must have been his mother's, he discovered a framed photograph tucked away in a bureau. It was a picture of his mother, Angela, holding him as a baby, and it bore out the housekeeper's theory that the room must have been hers. There was no doubt that Angela had been a beautiful woman, with glossy dark hair and vivid blue eyes, but it wasn't just her beauty that drew the viewer in. Her smiling face exuded warmth and love in equal measures as she held her son firmly against her heart.

How she must have hated being ill and unable to look after him, Gabriel thought.

The idea jolted him.

Up until now, Angela Devenish had been an almost ghost-like figure in his mind—hardly real. As if she'd never existed at all. Now her life and the woman she had been started to fascinate him. He studied the photograph for a long time. He even took it with him into his bedroom and stood it on the dressing table so that he would see it every morning when he woke up.

But even though he had begun to make genuine inroads into seeing his mother in a different light and healing the wounds from his past, there was one face that he longed to see again more than any other. And that face was Lara's.

The only thing that had held Gabriel back from going to see her when he'd returned to the UK was the sickening memory of how he had behaved towards her when they'd parted in New York. He also couldn't forget the story of how he'd rebuffed her when she'd been just sixteen at Sean's party. She hadn't had to elucidate how hurt she must have been. It had been written all over her face.

He honestly wouldn't blame her if when she saw him again she told him to go to hell. But he hoped to God she wouldn't. Until he had made the decision to live in his family's manor so that he could inherit—not so that he might sell the property but so that he could make it his home—he hadn't known how he could legitimately approach her. All he had known was that he wanted to show Lara that he could be a better man, a truly good man—a man she could depend on.

And to do that he would have to show her evidence that he intended to stay in the country and make his life there.

If Lara agreed—and it was a big *if*—she would be an absolutely vital and crucial element in helping Gabriel create the new life he wanted. A much happier and more fulfilling life than he had ever experienced before.

Three months later...

Lara pressed her palm to the base of her spine and rubbed it. Having been on her feet since the early hours of the morning, she was so tired she could drop. Why did her tiredness and stress always seem to go straight to her back these days? she wondered.

With a jolt, she remembered that she was pregnant. The realisation still came as a shock every time she thought about it, but it had all been confirmed by her doctor so there was no more doubting. It still seemed like the most unbelievable dream.

With a wistful sigh, Lara started to go through her usual routine of shutting up shop for the day. All she could think about now was the prospect of a long and leisurely soak in the tub with some scented bubbles. That should help ease the ache in her back.

'Any plans for the evening, Lara?' her young colleague Marisa asked as she shut down her computer beside her.

'Only to have the longest, most relaxing soak in history, in a bath full of deliciously warm and sudsy water.'

'Sounds heavenly.' Marisa smiled.

'What about you? Have you any plans?'

'I'm going out for a pizza with Mark, my boyfriend.'

'You're still seeing him? I thought you two had had a big row and you had decided not to see him any more.'

Marisa's plump cheeks suffused with heat. 'Every now and again we fall out. But we quickly patch things up.' She smiled. 'He's a nice boy. I'd miss him if we weren't together. Sometimes he feels like a missing part of me I didn't know I'd lost. Do you know what I mean?'

Lara *did* know what she meant, and helplessly she felt the other girl's comment catching her off guard. Her eyes filled with tears. The thought of Gabriel and the memory of his passionate caresses and kisses was never far away. Those memories were even more poignant now that she knew she was carrying his baby. Did he ever think about her and wonder how she was doing? Did he ever miss her?

It had been neither simple nor easy to slip back into the predictable routine of the life she'd had before he'd walked in and ignited all her hopes and dreams with a fierce burning light that would never go out. So far it had been the biggest challenge of her life. Lara wondered how Gabriel would react if he knew that. It all but killed her to think he might just brush it off and put it down to experience.

'Lara?' Stepping towards her, Marisa looked alarmed to see that she was weeping. 'What's wrong, love? Do you feel sick? Do you want me to get you a glass of water?'

She suddenly sounded much older than her years,

and the younger woman's concern made Lara want to weep even more.

Touching her fingertips to the moisture that had tracked down her face and dampened her cheeks, she shook her head and forced a smile. 'No, I'll be fine, thanks. I think I just need to get out of here and go home and have that bath.'

'That's bound to help. A long hot bath is a bit of a cure-all for me, too. It's the same as having a cup of tea, isn't it? It somehow makes you feel better.'

Marisa's sage remark had the effect of making Lara want to hug her—so she did. The other girl flushed with pleasure.

'You're wise beyond your years—you know that?' Lara told her. Then, moving away, she glanced over at all the empty chairs and tables that would be full of diligent and not so diligent students again tomorrow. One thing was for certain: life went on, despite what was happening in your personal life.

Reaching for the red wool cardigan she'd hung over the back of her chair, she hurriedly pulled it on. Lifting up the heavy swathe of hair that had fallen down her back she let it fall again and shook it free. Absently glancing towards the twin glass doors of the exit, she frowned. A man dressed in a classic raincoat thrown over a dark sweatshirt and jeans was pushing them open.

Stepping inside, he took a brief inventory of his surroundings before tunnelling his fingers through his hair and moving towards them. Even if she hadn't seen his face Lara would have known that smooth athletic gait anywhere. Staring in disbelief, she found it hard to think, never mind *speak*. In fact, she suddenly felt quite faint.

'Who could that be?' Marisa whispered next to her. 'Doesn't he know that we're closed?'

'His name is Gabriel Devenish.'

Still in shock, Lara knew her voice wasn't much above a whisper. But it was almost as if she'd had to say his name out loud in order to believe that he was there and not just a figment of her imagination, or some seductive ghostly visitation from one of her nightly dreams of him.

When he stepped up to the counter and turned the vivid azure beam of his too-arresting gaze on her, a well of hurt and long-suppressed fury at his cavalier treatment rose up inside her and made her stiffen her shoulders defensively.

Lifting her chin, she looked him straight in the eye and announced, 'We're closed. If you need any help I'm afraid you'll have to come back tomorrow.'

The beautiful carved lips in front of her edged into an amused smile—a smile that unscrupulously stormed Lara's heart and turned her insides to mush.

'I'm afraid what I need can't wait until tomorrow,' he remarked, and the smoky voice and piercing eyes mercilessly imprisoned her, locked her up and threw away the key.

For a long moment she fell into a kind of trance. Then the sound of Marisa pointedly clearing her throat behind her and touching her hand to Lara's sleeve had her turning round to see what was wrong.

There was nothing amiss. The younger girl's eyes were alive with curiosity and what might have even been delight as she commented, 'I'm sorry, Lara, but I have to dash. Mark is meeting me in the car park. Take care of yourself, won't you? I'll see you tomorrow.'

'Enjoy your pizza,' Lara murmured automatically.

As the twin glass doors swung shut behind the slender blonde, her heart hammered at the realisation that she and Gabriel were alone. The impulse to do something, *anything*, to help still her nerves took hold, but Gabriel's handsome face was suddenly looking ominously serious and she couldn't help but stare. Just what did he want to say to her? Whatever it was, she was determined that she would have her say first.

'What on earth are you doing here—and how did you know where to find me? I don't recall giving you the college's address.'

'I went to see your parents,' he replied. 'Your mother told me where to find you.'

'When was this?'

'This morning.'

Lara's hand automatically shot to her abdomen. She gently rubbed it through the soft grey tunic she wore beneath her cardigan, then realised she was drawing attention to the one place she didn't want Gabriel's eyes to be drawn to.

Had her mum told him about the pregnancy? Even though she had been over the moon on hearing Lara's news about the baby, declaring it was the blessing she had been praying for, Lara was confident that she wouldn't have told him anything without checking with her first. But her insides still churned at the thought of how Gabriel would take the news.

'Why did you go to see them? Was it to collect Sean's photographs? And when did you get back to the UK? Is this another flying visit, Gabriel?'

Seeing that Lara's slender hands were gripping the edge of the fibreglass counter as if her life depended on it, and hearing the distress in her voice, Gabriel frowned. He hated the idea that his appearance had upset her, even though he knew she had plenty of reason to be distressed. The need to alleviate her unhappiness became imperative.

'I'll explain everything in a moment. Trust me, there's nothing to worry about. Right now all I want to do is look at you.'

He ached with an unholy ache to take her in his arms and kiss away every hurt, every moment of unease or despair he had ever visited on her, but he forced himself to wait. This wasn't the moment to blunder back into her life and just take what he wanted as if it was his God-given right. That was the *old* Gabriel. The man who had been too selfish and self-obsessed to know what a gift had been bestowed on him when Lara had surrendered her virginity and confessed that she loved him—had *always* loved him.

'You look tired. The shadows under your eyes look like bruises and you're far too pale. What have you been doing to yourself? Burning the candle at both ends?'

Gabriel hadn't meant his observation to sound critical, but he saw straight away that Lara was immediately defensive—*angry*, too. Her animated reaction confirmed it.

'What do *you* care what I've been doing? You didn't even bother to ring me after I left New York, and nor did you have the decency to let me know you were back in the UK! I'm done with worrying about you, Gabriel. I really am. I think it's time I focused my attention on myself and my own needs.'

Her dark eyes crestfallen, she leant towards the desk

and switched off the lamp that was there. Then she opened a drawer and collected her shoulder bag.

'I'm going home now. It's been a long day.'

'We need to talk, Lara. I know you probably think I'm not worth giving the time of day to, but I want the opportunity to help change your mind about that. Did you drive here?'

'Yes, I did.'

'Then I'll follow you in my car.'

She didn't answer. With her head held high, and clutching her bag in front of her, she came round the counter and started to walk towards the exit.

Although she hadn't argued with his intention, Gabriel felt oddly hurt that she wouldn't even look at him. Instead she arranged the strap of her bag more firmly onto her shoulder and drew the sides of her long wool cardigan together as if she was cold. Almost as if needing to protect herself. Then she proceeded out of the building to the car park.

The journey back to Lara's flat was thankfully a short one. Afraid that too long a delay before they were able to talk would give her added time to mull over past events and decide she would be better off without him, Gabriel couldn't help but be anxious. She'd seemed so adamant just now that they were over. But then he remembered the times when she'd openly demonstrated how much she cared and once again hope flared inside him.

Standing beside her as she inserted the key in the lock and opened the door of the Victorian semi where she lived, he stayed silent as a reluctant Lara invited him in.

'We'll talk in the living room,' she declared, her

brown eyes issuing him with a mere cursory glance before sliding quickly away again. 'The sooner we get this over and done with, the better.'

In spite of its lofty ceiling, the room Gabriel followed Lara inside to was surprisingly cosy and welcoming. The space couldn't help but reflect the personal touches and preferences of the woman who lived there. From the small collection of family photographs that sat atop the pine bookcase and the mantelpiece to the several wooden shelves that were literally crammed with books, it was eminently clear what the occupant's priorities were.

A seriously comfortable-looking dark gold couch with an embroidered throw on the back was strewn with brightly coloured cushions, and an old Chesterfield armchair sat before an uncurtained window overlooking the garden.

'You may as well sit down.' Her tone less than inviting, Lara threw her shoulder bag down onto the couch and, with her arms folded, moved her head to indicate he take the armchair.

Murmuring 'Ladies first', Gabriel waited until his reluctant hostess had settled herself on the couch and then, shrugging off his raincoat, he folded it over the back of the venerable old armchair and sat down.

'You said you were going to explain everything?'

Her pretty face was inevitably troubled as she leant forward in her seat to study him. Sighing, Gabriel scraped his fingers through his thick dark hair and smiled. 'I will. What I want to tell you is that I decided what I wanted wasn't in New York after all, but here.'

'You mean your family's home? Have you decided to sell it?'

'I'm not just talking about the manor, Lara. Although in answer to your question I have to tell you I'm *not* intending on selling it. My plan is to live there. In fact I've been living there for the past three months now, attempting to make my peace with the past and turning the place back into a home—a *real* home.'

'You have? Oh, Gabriel, that's wonderful.'

The surprise and pleasure that shone from her beautiful dark eyes couldn't help but melt Gabriel's heart. But he hadn't finished telling her the full extent of his plans yet, and a lot depended on her answer to his next question as to whether he carried them out or not.

'The truth is, Lara…' he continued. 'The truth is it won't be a real home until you agree to marry me and come and live with me there. Will you?'

CHAPTER TWELVE

IT WASN'T THE MOST romantic thing in the world to have happen, but when the full impact of Gabriel's question hit her, Lara sensed a sudden, urgent need to be sick. Hurriedly rising to her feet, she threw him an apologetic look and ran out through the door to her bedroom's en-suite bathroom. Once there, she crouched down in front of the toilet and was violently ill even as she heard Gabriel come in behind her.

'Sweetheart, what's wrong?'

As his deeply concerned voice asked the question, he stooped down behind her and gently gathered her hair behind her head so that it wouldn't fall over her face. When she'd finished, it was to find him running some cold water into the sink and dampening a washcloth. Almost as if she was a little girl he proceeded to wipe her mouth, dabbing gently at her lips, and then he carefully helped her to her feet.

'Wait here,' he instructed, and as the familiar, warm, musky scent of his cologne besieged her senses and rendered her even weaker he briefly disappeared, to return with a glass of cold water. 'Take a good long drink,' he ordered her.

Although he patiently waited for her to finish, Lara easily sensed the concern that gripped him.

When she glanced up again Gabriel removed the glass from her trembling hands and stood it on the shelf above the sink. Then he stared at her. Many times before she had been the recipient of that intensely direct examination, but it had never been as intense as this. Disturbingly, what she saw in the depths of that glittering gaze were varying shades of anger—like the precursor to a storm—and deep, deep anguish and pain.

'What the hell is going on, Lara? You'd better tell me.'

'Haven't you guessed? Don't you know the signs?'

Suddenly overwhelmed with the situation, she shouldered past him into the bedroom. Once there, she dropped down onto the bed and brought her hands up to her face. Incredibly, Gabriel had just asked her to marry him. But was he now going to reject her because she was pregnant? She almost couldn't bear the thought. Before she knew it scalding tears were trickling down behind her palms.

Suddenly the door opened and Gabriel was there. He was staring down at her, a muscle flinching in the side of his carved cheekbone, his expression mirroring hurt disbelief.

'You're pregnant.'

It was a statement of fact, not a question. Raising her head, Lara met his accusing gaze with her heart thudding and her mouth as dry as sand. 'Yes. Yes, I am.'

'So no sooner had we parted than you found yourself another man? I thought I was getting to know you, Lara, but now I realise I didn't know you at all.'

Sounding despairing, Gabriel started to move back

towards the door, as if he had already made up his mind what he was going to do about her admission.

But then he turned and said furiously, 'You certainly didn't waste your time missing me, did you? And to think I believed you when you said you were a virgin the first time we made love. What a prize idiot I was to fall for such an unlikely story!'

With his hand on the doorknob he glared at Lara, then stalked from the room. Ice-cold fear poured through her like white-water rapids as she realised he was going to leave.

Lara jumped up and ran after him.

'Gabriel!'

She got to the living room just as he was collecting his coat from the back of the chair and she rushed forward to grab his wrist and stop him from going. Suddenly it was *her* turn to be furious.

'You *are* an idiot. Such a stupid, *stupid* idiot!' Even as the accusation left her lips a fresh bout of scalding tears rolled down her cheeks and Gabriel stared at her, clearly uncomprehending either her meaning or the reason for her distress. 'Do you honestly think I would sleep with another man when it's *you* that I love—have always loved and always will?'

His lip curled with disdain. 'But you've just admitted that you're pregnant.' He shook off her grip on his arm. 'Or are you going to try and convince me it was some kind of immaculate conception?'

Lara sucked in her breath in a bid to try and steady herself. 'Before you go any further I need to tell you—I need to tell you it's true that when we first slept together I was a virgin. I waited all these years to give up my virginity to a man I really loved because it was im-

portant to me. That man has always been you, Gabriel.'
She paused to take in another steadying breath and saw
the interplay of hope and uncertainty that crossed his
face. 'The baby is *yours*, Gabriel,' she finished.

'What?'

'Just hear me out, will you? I fell pregnant when I
forgot to take one of my contraceptive pills that week
we were together in New York. I didn't do it deliberately. I would never try and trap you like that. But
my head was in the clouds the whole time I spent
with you—it was like a dream. I only discovered I'd
missed one of my pills a few weeks after I got home.
I'd been feeling nauseous and light-headed, but I put
that down to being upset because I was missing you
and you hadn't been in touch. I didn't even know if I
would ever see you again.'

'The baby is mine?' The raincoat Gabriel was holding slid out of his hand onto the floor.

Raising her hand in an attempt to dry her tears, Lara
nodded. 'I swear it. I'll show you the foil packet with
the pill I didn't take still in it. You can trace it back to
our week together in New York. But if you still don't
believe me then I don't know how else to convince
you. I foolishly thought my word and the devotion I've
shown you would be enough. I don't tell lies, Gabriel.
Remember I told you that once before?'

The man standing in front of her looked seriously
stunned. 'Why didn't you tell me you were pregnant
as soon as you found out? I would have come back
straight away.'

Shrugging, Lara gave him a wobbly smile. 'I didn't
want to put any pressure on you or make you feel ob-
ligated, that's why. I especially didn't want that be-

cause of the way you were when we said goodbye at
the airport. You seemed so angry, Gabriel. Angry and
distant. It was as though you resented me. I knew you
were already in turmoil because of your uncle's letter
and what he'd told you about your mother. I didn't want
to add to your worries.'

Gabriel was shaking his head as if he couldn't quite
believe what he was hearing. 'You really are unbelievable—you know that? You had every damn right in the
world to demand I come back and take up my responsibility to you and the baby. When will you learn that
you're the important one, Lara—not me?'

'Don't say that. You're very important to me, too,
Gabriel.' She followed this declaration with a puzzled
frown. 'But why didn't you tell me you'd decided to
come back and live at the manor? Were you thinking
that I would automatically expect us to take up where
we left off when you clearly had doubts about our relationship?'

'You crazy woman,' he breathed.

Fastening his hands around her slim upper arms, he
pulled her against his chest. Lara's heart went wild. As
he pushed back a stray curl where it brushed against
the side of her cheek she saw his intimate smile was
candid and unguarded as he gazed back at her, and it
rendered him even more beautiful in her eyes. That
heartrending smile suggested he'd made the decision
to reveal at last the *real* Gabriel Devenish. To reveal
the honourable and decent man behind the steely corporate facade and the much admired financial acu-
ity that he was known for. The man Lara had always
known he was.

'I didn't want to tell you I was coming back to live

at the manor until I'd taken some proper time to examine some of the hurts from my past and tried to make some headway into healing them. You didn't deserve to be with a broken man, Lara—a man who didn't know how to love anyone but himself.'

He grimaced painfully.

'And I didn't even make a very convincing job of that. I poured all my energies into my work, and my relentless desire to be the best at what I did was only because I wanted to have the admiration and praise of my peers. I was looking for validation that I was worthwhile. It wasn't even about the money. But that ambition became the most important thing in my life. A very empty and meaningless life, when all was said and done.

'Apart from being good at my job, I didn't regard myself as being good at very much at all. And I didn't have meaningful relationships because I couldn't allow myself to be close to a woman in case I was betrayed in some way—that's another reason why I directed all my attention into my work.

'And as far as doubts are concerned, I can tell you that the only doubts I had were whether I was good enough to be with an angel like you,' he continued huskily. 'I always intended on coming back for you, Lara. Was I hoping for too much when I hoped that you would want to share the rest of your life with a man like me? As I want to share my life with you?'

Lara lifted her hand to lay her palm gently against his roughened cheek. 'No,' she said earnestly. 'You weren't hoping for too much. I can't think of anything I'd like more than to share the rest of my life with you. Besides…no one else would want me if I couldn't be with you Gabriel. I'd be like an empty shell. Don't you know that you've ruined me for any other man because my body and soul belongs to you?'

A profoundly dazed look stole into the eyes that gazed back at her.

Gabriel's hands tightened as they dropped down to her hips and pulled her harder against him. 'And now you're going to have my baby. I'm going to be a father. *We* are going to be parents, with a family of our own. I can't help asking myself if I deserve to be this happy.'

'So you don't mind that we'll have a baby to take care of so early in our relationship? We can't pretend it won't be challenging.'

'We'll weather any storms that come, sweetheart,' Gabriel reassured her warmly. 'We'll weather them because together we're strong and our love won't let the challenges of life overwhelm us. Look at what we've already overcome. This baby will bring us ever closer—just you wait and see.'

His face came towards hers, but with a quick shake of her head Lara gently but firmly pushed him away. 'You have to let me go and freshen my mouth before you kiss me,' she declared. 'Then I'll let you kiss me senseless if you want!'

His carved lips quirked in an amused grin. 'That's like asking me if I need to take my next breath. If you take longer than ten seconds then I'm coming to find you—and I warn you…if you're not ready there'll be a hell of a penalty to pay.' As she smiled and walked towards the door, he added, 'And you still haven't answered my question.'

Feigning ignorance, Lara stopped and turned to examine him. 'What question might that be?'

'Will you marry me? Put me out of my misery, woman, and give me your answer. A man can only take so much before he cracks.'

Her expression softening, Lara laid her hand over her heart and then, with a graceful flourish, indicated that it was his. 'Of course I'll marry you, Gabriel. That's always been my intention—ever since Sean brought you home with him that very first time. He'll be so pleased that two of the people he loved best are going to be together, don't you think?'

It was as she turned and left the room that Gabriel finally realised fully the immense capacity to love that Lara had. Sean had possessed that capacity, too. Shaking his head, he didn't even try and stem the tears that welled in his eyes.

His head was spinning. The woman he loved had agreed to be his wife and she was pregnant with their baby. All the things Gabriel had thought would be denied him were coming true.

He already knew that his future goals didn't have anything to do with continuing to be a 'mover and shaker' on Wall Street, but were to do with being a loving husband and father, with his children growing up happy and content with two parents who adored them and who would do everything in their power to help them have a wonderful life. And they would all live together in the beautiful manor house that Gabriel had inherited from his family. Uncle Richard's heartfelt hope was going to be realised.

The architects and designers Gabriel had hired were already helping him bring his home into the twenty-first century without encroaching on the Regency building's historic innate beauty and grace, and he was already pleased with some of the results they had achieved. Lara had agreed that she was, too, and the room that had given them both the most pleasure was the beautiful nursery—although Lara was already insisting that the baby would share their room until she was confident that he or she was ready to sleep in a room by themselves.

Suddenly aware that the small gathering behind him in the glass-ceilinged conservatory had fallen into a reverent silence, and knowing that Lara's parents were closest to them at the front of the seated rows, he brought his mind right back to the present and the radiant and beautiful woman at his side.

Lara looked absolutely stunning in her simple but elegant wedding gown. It was fashioned in lavender-coloured floor-length satin and her mother, Peggy, had helped her decide on it. It was the perfect choice for her daughter's timeless beauty. The strapless design had a sweetheart neckline and a beaded appliqué underneath the bust, and the material flowed down over the waist that five months of pregnancy had clearly but not yet too obviously swelled.

His clasp on her slender hand tightened a little possessively as Lara lifted her shimmering dark eyes to his. For a man who had prided himself on addressing many corporate banquets and dinners with aplomb, Gabriel suddenly found himself bereft of words.

Clearing his throat, he leant towards his bewitching wife-to-be and asked in hushed tones, 'Are you ready for this? You don't want to change your mind?'

Momentarily taken aback, Lara blinked. Then her soft pink-painted lips curved in a loving, amused smile.

'Are you serious? To use an often used cliché, for which I won't apologise, I've been waiting for this moment all my life.'

Gabriel chuckled and claimed her lips in a briefly hungry kiss that he had no intention of apologising for, either. When he looked up again the professional celebrant who stood in front of them—a slender woman with copper-coloured hair and merry brown eyes—bestowed an indulgent smile upon them and reprimanded him teasingly.

'You're meant to kiss the bride when I pronounce that you're man and wife, Mr Devenish, *not* before!'

Unable to resist, Gabriel remarked, 'No offence, but nobody tells me when I can and can't kiss the woman I love—the woman I adore more than life itself.'

Briefly stunned into silence, the celebrant bestowed another smile on him. Then, her gaze encompassing both him and Lara, she said, 'Shall we proceed with the ceremony now?'

Unable to stop himself from having the last word, Gabriel twined his fingers with Lara's and answered, 'Trust me, I'm as anxious to get the ceremony under way and make this amazing woman my wife as you are!'

There was a delighted ripple of laughter from behind them at that declaration, and a gently respectful round of applause. As for Lara—she glanced up at the handsome blue-eyed man at her side, dressed in a flawless midnight blue tuxedo, and offered up a silent prayer of thanks for her great good fortune.

Then the voice of her brother stole into her mind, saying, *'I always told you to go for what you wanted in life, and that if you wanted it enough you would get it...remember?'*

Swallowing back her tears, Lara murmured under her breath, 'Yes, Sean, I remember—and you were right. Thank you.'

* * * * *

A sneaky peek at next month...

MODERN™

POWER, PASSION AND IRRESISTIBLE TEMPTATION

My wish list for next month's titles...

In stores from 20th June 2014:

❏ Christakis's Rebellious Wife — Lynne Graham

❏ Carrying the Sheikh's Heir — Lynn Raye Harris

❏ Dante's Unexpected Legacy — Catherine George

❏ The Ultimate Playboy — Maya Blake

In stores from 4th July 2014:

❏ At No Man's Command — Melanie Milburne

❏ Bound by the Italian's Contract — Janette Kenny

❏ A Deal with Demakis — Tara Pammi

❏ Wrong Man, Right Kiss — Red Garnier

Available at WHSmith, Tesco, Asda, Eason, Amazon and Apple

Just can't wait?

Visit us Online

You can buy our books online a month before they hit the shops! **www.millsandboon.co.uk**

0614/01

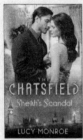   

THE

CHATSFIELD®

Enter the intriguing online world of
The Chatsfield and discover secret
stories behind closed doors...

www.thechatsfield.com

Check in online now for your exclusive
welcome pack!

The World of Mills & Boon

There's a Mills & Boon® series that's perfect for you. There are ten different series to choose from and new titles every month, so whether you're looking for glamorous seduction, Regency rakes, homespun heroes or sizzling erotica, we'll give you plenty of inspiration for your next read.

By Request
Back by popular demand!
12 stories every month

Cherish
Experience the ultimate rush of falling in love.
12 new stories every month

INTRIGUE...
A seductive combination of danger and desire...
7 new stories every month

Desire
Passionate and dramatic love stories
6 new stories every month

nocturne
An exhilarating underworld of dark desires
3 new stories every month

For exclusive member offers go to
millsandboon.co.uk/subscribe

Which series will you try next?

Join the Mills & Boon Book Club

Want to read more **Modern**™ books?
We're offering you **2 more** absolutely **FREE!**

We'll also treat you to these fabulous extras:

- **Exclusive offers and much more!**
- **FREE home delivery**
- **FREE books and gifts with our special rewards scheme**

Get your free books now!

visit www.millsandboon.co.uk/bookclub
or call Customer Relations on 020 8288 2888